MYTHS
OF GODS

A Tale of What Always Has
Been and Never Will Be

MYTHS OF GODS

A Tale of What Always Has Been and Never Will Be

Leigh M. Lane

CEREBRAL BOOKS
Missoula, MT

DEDICATION

This book is dedicated to all those who believe in and deny God, to those who have faith and those who are uncertain, to those who love religion and those who despise it, and to all those who question what humanity has made of it all.

ACKNOWLEDGMENTS

Special thanks to Thomas Lane and Kathryn Sirls, without whom this novel would never have come to be what it is today. Thanks to Shirlee Whitcomb, whose support has both molded my work and tempered my soul. Thanks to Dana Fredsti and David Fitzgerald, whose insights helped to shape the final face of this work. Thanks to Erin Barker, Keri Rae Boyle and Lauren Yellon, whose honesty made a difference greater than they know. And finally, thank you, Dad, for believing in me.

CONTENTS

Prologue
THE BEGINNING

At first, thought had been marginal, nearly negligible. There had been no words, no images. Thought simply had been. Then, somewhere amongst the nothingness had come a chaotic activation of awareness—a great epiphany: *I am.*

This filled me with delight. I became aware of my thoughts and decided that to be was a marvelous thing. Delight quickly gave way to an overwhelming sense of curiosity, however, when I needed to ask, *What does it mean to be?* Lacking any information with which to weigh the question, the only logical route was to explore the opposing concept, *not* to be. I considered the only explanation, given what little I knew: *To be is what I am; what is not I is that which does not exist.*

I contemplated the possibility that I had not always been. Conversely, if I had not always been, I had to have come from somewhere. Reasoning that nothing else existed outside of me, and that I could not have been made to exist if there had been nothing to create me, the only valid conclusion was that I had always existed. Why I had not always been aware of my being I was only able to speculate.

I found moments every so often when I recalled my great epiphany, and the ecstasy of discovering my existence would return. The excitement would last for so long, however, and then the questions would reappear, which would lead to a newfound sense of emptiness. Sometimes I felt as if the agony would never end, which eventually forced me to acknowledge *time*.

With the acknowledgment of time, I realized I possessed a past I could recall but could never change. I always existed in the present, and the present was nothing more than a series of moments that were all soon to become bits of past, themselves. Strangely, however, although I was able to recollect previous thoughts, I was unable to foresee the future. I wondered, with great trepidation, how long time also had existed without my recognition. Time had made me grow restless, and time would continue . . .

Forever?

I began to ponder this new concept with worry and dejection. If there had never been a beginning, then it had only stood to reason that there would also be no end. My emptiness soon became all-consuming, my restlessness slowly growing to the point of being unbearable.

I do not want to be, I finally thought.

That made no difference. I continued to be, and time continued on. I long had lost the delights of past wonders, left now with nothing but agony and agitation. I wondered if time knew of my existence.

Had it possibly been cognizant of the torment it caused me?

But what is time? How did it come to exist? These seemed impossible questions to answer, but I knew that I needed not acknowledge time for it to exist. I pondered the nature of my existence, compared it to the existence of time, and then considered their relationship. The ecstasy returned when I realized that time was not a separate entity, but rather a part of me. Time existed because I existed.

I realized that I was not simply that which existed; *I was all that existed, including time*—and there was more. With an unexpected burst, I broke through the constraints of my own nothingness, manifesting the opposite. I became aware of space, and with that, I discovered yet another part of me I had not previously been aware of: *energy*, which in turn I could condense into *matter*. I delighted in the amazing new possibilities that this presented, as I realized I didn't have to exist forever in the torment of simply pondering my existence. *To be* could mean so much more.

I began with the most basic elements of myself, which I had found I could piece together with interesting results. At first, my creations were rudimentary and simplistic. I experimented with the elements, mixing them in random ways, until I developed an understanding of which ones pieced together well and which ones did not. As I created all sorts and sizes of matter, I learned how to manipulate the arrangements into inventions of countless makes and attributes. My first objects, simple spheres of matter, had been interesting enough for a while, although I had not yet determined if there could be any practical use for them.

I learned to will the matter to perform races and other entertaining tricks. Curious to know the effect, I caused several spheres to collide, discovering the intriguing new sensation of *destruction*. Just as easily as an object could be molded and developed, it could be crushed, distorted, or completely annihilated. With this simple invention, I also found that nothing I created had the ability to last for very long. All physical things degraded, and everything I carefully constructed eventually became nothing more than dust littering my space.

I soon decided that, as interesting as it was to see the destruction of old things, I also craved to create things that might last long enough to enjoy for a time. I focused on creations that could self-perpetuate, while continuing to experiment with different attributes that might assist me further in my quest for self-discovery. I discovered that there was a distinctive part of me that I could use to add better longevity to my creations. Unexpectedly, this also caused objects to become, to varying degrees, animated, which both surprised and excited me. I began to focus on these interesting new beings, experimenting with their attributes and seeing what different entertaining behaviors I might make them capable of exhibiting.

There came the first hints of *life*, elemental beings: elegant, flowing hot spheres dancing in fiery spirals, always changing, reveling in the sensation of being physical. The fiery spheres had been a magnificent breakthrough. Not only did they exist for much longer than anything else I had created, capable of self-sustaining for vast stretches of time, but they also spontaneously triggered a set of very specific and beautiful natural laws I had not anticipated. They required additional substances in order to sustain themselves, which had been interesting in itself, but what was even more fascinating was their conversion of these substances, which in turn created new elements I could use as building blocks for even more complex objects.

Space become a series of systems and chain reactions, chaotic in some places and uniform in others, but altogether capable of enabling objects to exist in innumerable ways and for much longer spans. The fluidity and grace the small universe had suddenly taken on pleased me immensely, and I focused on how I might improve upon the finer details and expand my experiments.

Sometime during that seemingly endless span, I came to recognize and identify a feeling of loneliness. This had only intensified the longer I was aware of it, and so I decided to set out on a quest to recreate true sentience. *If I am capable of creating objects and simple beings, can I not also create companions for myself?* Unsure if such a feat was even possible, I decided that a comprehensive experiment was in order.

I contemplated the different approaches I might take in the operation and considered animating a number of tiny spheres of various materials, simple creatures that could roll across the variable terrain created on the larger, orbiting spheres. The tiny spheres would be able to experience different things depending on where they rolled, which would be fun and informative enough for at least a while, and perhaps we might even come to some means of interacting on a meaningful level. A final streak of inspiration struck me, however, and I decided to take a more imaginative approach—surely, I could think of something more creative to animate than simple, droning spheres. I struggled at first to come up with ideas, without any muse of stimuli or association to feed my thoughts, and my initial ideas were basic and almost as simplistic as the elementals.

The organisms were minute in size, yet they had difficulty negotiating their terrain. I experimented with various substrates and happened upon a fluidic compound, which proved to be easier to navigate than the planet's otherwise solid environment. I released the tiny creatures into their hot, more navigable new habitat, gratified with the result. The organisms were able to move quickly through the compound, and they were able to perform simple tricks such as spins and twirls. They were entertaining to watch but, much to my dismay, the tiny organisms, like the elementals, proved incapable of acknowledging their own existence—or mine.

I decided to try my luck with larger organisms by piecing together clusters of the smaller ones, considering the possibility that complexity might be the missing piece to my puzzle. Through trial and error, I pieced together complex organisms that swam, flew, walked, slithered, and crawled. I discovered that at a certain size, lifeforms required a control center for their various physical functions. In many of those lifeforms, that control center also coincidentally solved the problem of sentience and complex thought. As the thoughts of my new amazing creations began to course through me, a second, vicarious level of existence arose through the discovery of organic thought.

I discovered physical touch, the different sensations of feeling, and I experimented with the various pleasures and horrors they had offered. Shortly thereafter, there came the discovery of sight, which brought forth the rich delights of light and color. By willing the existence of living, thinking beings, I found that I was able to experience secondhand sensations that went beyond even my own imaginings. Life was not just a new level of existence, but rather *the key to existence itself.*

I had observed all of the beings for some time when I finally determined that, with a seemingly ever-growing level of intelligence, the lovely and curious bipeds showed the most promise for further development. I spent much time trying to determine how best to mold these interesting beings into my own educational tools, and I granted the beings as much intelligence as their beautiful little minds could handle.

Together, we will now discover the meaning of existence, I thought, hopeful.

Chapter I
THE OMNISCIENT ONE

"**Y**ou must listen!" cried the wild-eyed philosopher. He gestured with his free hand to a book cradled in the crook of his other arm. The thin, timeworn volume was leather-bound and held together with a metal clasp.

Only a handful of people surrounded the man, but they stood in eager silence, waiting for him to continue. He told them how the book had opened his mind to ideas their leaders wanted to keep concealed, claiming that the Elders' One True God was a manufactured scheme used to control the masses. He went on to declare that God, finding their religious ideals both flattering and sad, planned on sending five prophets into the wombs of five virgins, divine ambassadors who would forge a genuine bridge between Man and Creator and set the people straight. The people would know they were on their way when the eleven planets aligned and a solar eclipse turned the world dark.

The small audience looked among one another for denial or support, a light murmur of voices passing between them.

He carefully opened the book and pointed to a page that indicated religious difference was what caused God to create the Dead Lands. It was a symptom of their own destructive nature, and was meant to wipe them out completely. He leafed further through the book then read aloud, "The people cried out to be spared, desperate, and eventually God answered their prayers. Before the last of the land went dead, God halted the Dead Lands' expansion and willed water and fertile soil wherever live land remained. While humankind rejoiced, God decided the only option was to teach them directly what they needed to know."

The philosopher shut the book as the group turned to the sound of armored guards approaching. A cloaked man, the Head Elder, walked ahead of them.

"God will come to the people in the form of three boys and two girls," the philosopher continued, already bracing for the attack. "Watch for them and heed their leadership!"

"Deceiver! Heathen!" the Elder cried.

"Watch and listen!" the philosopher yelled as the guards broke through the audience. He hugged the book to his chest as a sword moved to impale him. The thin blade slid through the leather binding, past the volume of handwritten pages, and into his heart, forcing him to his knees. He gasped his final breaths as his audience scattered and the guards surrounded him.

"Tell me where to find the other copies!" the Elder demanded.

The philosopher looked down, watching his blood

slowly saturate the Holy Book now fixed to his chest with the guard's blade. He tried to speak, a pained cry escaping him instead, then he collapsed, his arms still clasped desperately around the warm, wet book.

"The Holy Tablets have warned us against false prophets," the Elder said as his guards carried away the philosopher and his book.

A townswoman gasped, pointing up at the sky. "Look!"

The people looked up as the moon slowly moved to block the sun.

"Assemble the people!" the Elder ordered. He turned to the growing audience. "It's a test of faith!"

Whispers moved through the crowd.

"But what about the rest of the prophecy?" a young man asked. "What about the prophets?"

"It's a false prophecy. Indeed, five virgins will conceive on this day," the Head Elder answered. "However, their children, if allowed to be born, will not be mankind's savior, but instead its destruction."

The townspeople fell silent, fear slowly taking over disbelief.

"The demonic children need to be destroyed before their mothers are able to unleash them unto the world. We need to discover them now, before it's too late!"

The people looked amongst one another as a shadow descended over them and everything went ominously dark. Avani Khess, a young and virtuous woman, noticed a light fall upon her. She searched all around in a panic, realizing, strangely, that no one else seemed to notice.

"Surely there must be someone you suspect!" the

Elder bellowed, his words echoing through the darkness. "Speak now, or be damned!"

Through the growing murmur, a young man spoke up: "My betrothed is in allegiance with the heathens, I'm sure of it!"

"Liar!" the young woman shrieked.

The Head Elder waved the man on. "Bring her forward!"

The young woman tried to flee, but the surrounding guards overtook her and dragged her before the Elder.

"It's not true!" she cried.

"Then why did you run?" the Elder asked.

She shook her head as she burst into tears. "My betrothed is in love with another woman! He's a liar and a cheat!" She looked over at her accuser, and he turned away, instead looking down in shame.

The growing crowd fell into a collective murmur of doubt and condemnation.

"Four more!" the Elder yelled. "Speak now, or the darkness will consume us all!"

Avani stepped aside, unable to hold back her tears as the accusations began to fly all around her. Somehow, no one noticed her guilty affect. No one suspected her. No one else saw the light that had filled her. No one else knew the truth.

By the time the daylight returned in full, five virgins stood before the collective Eldership and their guards. The rest of the town helped to gather firewood as they made their way to the sacrificial pyres.

The five women burned as the entire town watched. The women howled and shrieked as the flames licked their toes and danced up their legs. Their screams fell on deaf ears, echoing out through a sea of silent, staring eyes. The women screamed until they were no more, and then their audience began to walk away, leaving the sizzling, smoldering bodies to rot in the day's sun.

Jeza Khess sat up with a start, her body glazed with panicked sweat. She looked around her tiny bedroom, reminding herself of where she was, and with a deep breath, she got up and moved to the washroom.

She worked the indoor water pump and splashed her face, then looked at herself in the mirror. She was a tiny woman, seemingly fragile, but in fact exceptionally strong both in body and in will. She looked deep into her brilliant hazel eyes, which, viewed up close, seemed to contain every color possible, searching within for some greater truth. She pulled her hair into a long braid and got dressed. Like every other common woman, she wore a plain skirt kept hemmed at the ankles under a pale, threadbare smock. She moved barefoot to the modest farmhouse's front porch, where she found Avani enjoying a glass of cool water as she watched the sun rise.

Avani proved to be well-suited to bear and raise a deity such as Jeza. She offered her the respect and reverence she deserved, even when Jeza had been a child, when Avani undertook on the role of mother and humble servant. Jeza played the role of Avani's daughter with great pleasure and grace. For the first few years, she even went so far as to address Avani as

"Mommy," allowing the woman to coddle and care for her. By her fifth birthday, she had assumed a role closer to that of Avani's equal, although she did not fully give up her position as *the child* until closer to adolescence. Such a mixing of roles was often confusing for Avani, although she understood well enough to follow without question the child's every lead.

The two kept a small farm that sustained them comfortably, and Jeza spent most of her days working the land and tending to the livestock. Her mother maintained a grain and vegetable field, which provided the ingredients to most of their meals. They had a small orchard where they grew a few different varieties of fruit, most of which they sold in order to pay their tithe to the Elders. A small, free-roaming herd of livestock provided the two with milk and an occasional roast. Running a farm demanded heavy labor, but they both took pride in the modest fruits of their efforts and enjoyed their busy lives.

Jeza joined Avani on their porch. A refreshing breeze moved through the warm spring air. Hues of pink and purple lined the clouds along the horizon.

Avani turned away from the sunrise to assess the worry fixed upon Jeza's face. "Are you thinking or listening?" she asked.

"Both."

"Care to share?" Avani asked.

Jeza sighed. "You and I . . . we've spent a great deal of time discussing the nature of things." She shook her head. "It seems to me that we're both excellent at raising questions, but far stretched to find any answers."

Avani nodded, unsure how to respond.

"I've lived in this body for thirty-two years, and it has been a surreal experience. Thirty-two years—a mere moment in infinity—has become for me a massive slice of eternity." She shifted her full attention to the sunrise. "But it has been beautiful."

"So why so troubled this morning?"

Jeza swallowed hard. "I had another nightmare."

"I see."

"I have told myself that, perhaps if I waited long enough, the others might come to remember who they are." Jeza looked down. "The longer I wait, though, the clearer it becomes that's not going to happen. I fear we're losing ourselves more and more each day."

Avani placed a hand on Jeza's shoulder, but said nothing.

"I'm afraid that if I wait much longer, this body— this mind—it might consume me, as well." Jeza thought back to when she was the unbodied consciousness, and how God had not considered the possibility that the manifested beings would be so wholly human and unforeseeably flawed. Unlike the others, Jeza knew who she was from the moment God had willed her physical beginning. As the years passed by, she struggled more and more with the memories she had brought with her from before her conception. She knew everything that one could possibly know, and from time to time, it felt like too much for her tiny human mind to process.

The thoughts of every living creature, from the simplest of insects to the most complex of humans, sat in her mind, stored and easily accessed as if catalogued and preserved in an ever-growing private database. Just like the unbodied consciousness, however, she could not foresee the future. Even more frustrating was that, despite her constant omniscient processing and storing of thoughts, Jeza found great difficulty in trying to make sense of it all. Although she embodied the mind of God, the human mind in which it now resided was too simple to allow her to understand adequately all to which she had access. Moreover, it was the individual motivations and behaviors that invariably caused her confusion. From time to time, she would catch herself in a fit of anger, impatient or frustrated with those around her, unable to understand their ignorance. Rarely, even she took part in human quarrels, and she would have to take a moment to remind herself who she really was—and how petty the dispute, any dispute, really was.

Jeza shook her head. "I feel lost."

"Everyone does sometimes. That's just part of being human."

Jeza took another deep breath. She knew that the time drew near for her to make her move. Sadly, she knew that she would have to convince the other four of their parts in the plan before they could begin. Given the lives they each had grown to know, her task was not going to be easy. Most of them had been raised to worship humanity's "One True God." One of them had even been raised by an Elder. The unbodied consciousness had not considered the extent that interpersonal human dynamics might have played against them, and Jeza feared more and more that the experiment might quite possibly fail just because of that one unanticipated complication.

"The five of us are going to need to set up camp in

the Dead Lands soon," Jeza said, breaking a long silence between the two.

"The five of you?" Avani asked, trying to pretend she wasn't shocked or surprised. "How long will you be gone?"

"I don't know."

"Will you need me to supply you with anything?"

Jeza nodded. "We'll need some basic provisions."

"Can I come with you?" Avani asked, her throat tight as she considered what was to come.

Jeza hugged her, the feel of the woman's pain hitting her as strongly as if it her were hers alone to bear. "I would never leave you behind, my dear friend."

Avani nodded her thanks. She wiped the tears from her eyes and took a deep and calming breath.

"We both have much work we need to do before we can leave," Jeza said.

Avani nodded. "Just tell me what to do."

"Start collecting basics: blankets, non-perishables, water. Keep a low profile. Don't worry about getting more than just a few days' essentials; we can always return for more provisions once we have the camp set up."

Avani nodded.

"The Elders are watching the people more carefully than you think," Jeza continued. "They know we're here, and they look forward to taking us on."

"A little arrogant, don't you think?" Avani asked.

Jeza shrugged. "We are all arrogant in our own ways, some of us more than others. Only time will tell which of us holds humanity's fate."

Chapter II
ELDER KLOSIK

Elder Klosik, the senior officer of the people on both secular and religious matters, took his time at the breakfast table, enjoying the meal his wife had prepared. Lauru was a good woman and a humble wife, although they were sure the dark forces had cursed her barren—a deed the Elder insisted was in retaliation against his lifetime spent studying and enforcing the ancient Holy Tablets.

The Klosiks had been blessed with a child despite the supposed curse, however, when the Elder's own sister, Nalia, had to be put to death. Klosik had deemed her a whore when he had learned of her hidden daughter, but the want of a child had forced him to overlook any other possibilities behind the child's conception. The family had avoided close contact with him during the pregnancy, which was not difficult given his heavy load of responsibilities; however, they made the mistake of inviting him back home for a dinner in his honor a few months after his niece's birth, telling him that his mother, not his sister, had given birth to the child. He believed he had a new sister, taken by the ploy until Nalia's breasts, not their mother's, leaked milk upon the baby's cry.

Elder Klosik's parents had backed Nalia when she had presented to the Eldership a story about a masked rapist coming into her room one night and causing the pregnancy. When Nalia refused to indict anyone (even after Klosik privately told her that, if necessary, she could pick any innocent man), the Elder was left with no one to charge but Nalia. He could not take exception to family, he had reasoned. Nalia had engaged in non-marital intercourse, and he had no choice but to sentence his dear sister to the stake. All of the other Elders agreed it had been a noble move on his part, one of many actions that eventually moved Klosik into the position of Head Elder. Nalia's daughter, Vara, knew only Lauru and the Elder as her parents. She grew up a well-groomed, humble servant of the Eldership and people, the perfect godly daughter.

Elder Klosik and his wife lived in a large two-story brick and mortar manor. They housed a number of servants and lobotomized concubines, all of whom the Eldership paid for in full. Lauru insisted on doing the majority of the housework, leaving only the dirtiest jobs for the servants, and she cooked all of her husband's meals.

Breakfast this day had been, as usual, culinary perfection. The Elder and his wife both still wore their nightgowns, allowing themselves a slow and relaxing morning.

Lauru had already finished eating, and now read the morning newsletter.

"Anything interesting?" he asked.

She glanced at the various headlines and looked up with a shrug. "I'm sure there's nothing here that you don't already know."

"One can only hope."

Lauru set down the flimsy, one-page document, properly addressing her husband. "Did you finish your sermon?"

"I think so. If you want to look it over, it's in my study."

"I'll read it after I've cleaned up breakfast." Lauru stood, kissed her husband on the forehead, and began to clear the table.

One of the servants hurried into the room. She carried a small envelope. "Elder Klosik, sir, a messenger just dropped this off!" Suspecting that the messenger would have delivered the letter himself had the news not been dreadful, the servant set the envelope on the table in front of Elder Klosik and hurried out with a bow.

Elder Klosik nervously broke the envelope's wax seal. A horrified gasp escaped him as he read the message.

Lauru set down the dirty breakfast dishes, alarmed by the sudden paleness that had overtaken her husband's face. "What's wrong?"

"I'm to go to the Worship Hall immediately. The Holy Tablets have been destroyed!" He clenched the message in his hand, crushing it and the envelope into a small, crumpled mass. He stood, faltering over his seat for a moment as if he might faint.

Lauru pressed him for the mangled parchment, and he handed it to her. She quickly read the message and allowed him to comfort her as she began to cry. They embraced, crying together.

He kissed her on the forehead. "I've got work to do," he said, then called for his servants as he left for his robe room.

Servants helped him don his formal robe, a heavy uniform that covered his entire body from the chin down. Made out of a thick, expensive material, it was adorned with jewels and intricate embroidery. An elegant yet cumbersome show of wealth and status, all five Elders wore their robes whenever they were not in the privacy of their own homes. Over his robe, he wore a heavy, white sash, which both Elders and their spouses displayed across their chests at all times to signify their position of righteousness and privilege.

Elder Klosik grabbed a piece of fruit to eat on his way to the Worship Hall, and sent for a guarded cart to transport him. The simple two- or four-seated cart, which could be drawn by either livestock or two men, was a luxury that only the Elders could afford. The common people often used smaller carts, but usually to transport goods rather than themselves. Further, while an Elder or Elder's spouse traveling by cart was considered an exercise in privilege, a common person seen in a cart was considered lazy. The carts also served a more practical purpose, though, given the distance between each of the Elders' estates and the town square and Worship Hall, allowing them to make the two- to three-mile trip sometimes multiple times a day without undue hardship.

The Elders assembled at the Worship Hall and quickly organized a meeting with the common people. The massive congregation room could hold roughly a thousand people, and its tall, domed ceiling reverberated the Elders' voices as they spoke or sang. Tall marble pillars supported the dome, and stained glass images of Elders from past generations seemed to scrutinize all who entered through tall, colorful windows.

Messengers went to every home, and over the course of the next two hours, the people slowly filed in. Klosik stood, the rest of the Elders seated behind him, as he addressed the mass of distraught citizens.

"Our people," he began, and then waited for the din of voices to die off. "It is true that the Holy Tablets have been destroyed."

There was an immediate uproar. People cried out, damning their unseen enemies with angry and mournful words.

"The heathen terrorists have not won any battle, though," Elder Klosik continued, "because I had the tablets memorized—all of them. So, you see, they have not been destroyed at all."

The people began to cheer.

Elder Klosik continued: "We already have leads on the monsters behind this atrocity. I assure you that I will personally make sure they pay for what they've done."

The large room began to echo with cheers and applause.

The four other Elders, two men and two women, stood, joining Klosik. They watched over the people as the collection plates began their rounds. The people gave generously that day, giving more than their required shares, feeling grateful to be blessed with such a devoted and astute leader. The collection plates grew heavy with small spheres of different valued precious metals, which the people used in formal trade and to pay their monthly tithes. Green copper spheres were worth the most, their currency enough to cover a single adult's tithe. Silver was worth half of copper's value and covered child and adolescent tithes, while gold was worth a third of a silver sphere and paid infant tithes. For this reason, although the spheres were also valid currency in all other forms of trade, the people called them tithestones.

Elder Forese, an older woman, began to sing a hymn. Her powerful voice echoed through the cavernous room, and the people paused to listen for a moment before they joined her in her song. Soon, the room filled with the harmonies of a thousand voices. The people sang as one, heartfelt and exuberant, their voices carrying a message of unity and servitude to their One True God. The people sang until the Elders finished collecting the donation plates and opened the doors. The afternoon light poured in as the people filed out, one by one, to return to their homes and reflect upon the Elder's sermon.

The Elders locked up the Worship Hall, then met in their private chamber to discuss their current leads. The room was small, but lavishly furnished. Bowls of fruit and flasks of hard cider sat in the center of a semicircle-shaped wooden table, and five plush thrones adorned with carvings and fine jewels sat along one side. Elder Klosik's, the largest and most intricately decorated, sat in the center.

The Elders sat in silence for some time, setting

aside their worry temporarily with food and drink as they sorted and counted the month's tithe. When they were finished, they divided the tithestones and filled their purses, then set aside their cups and waited for Elder Klosik to speak.

"Any leads?" he finally asked.

Elder Forese cleared her throat. "I received a tip that Adtom Rudin, the carpenter's son, was seen near the vault just before the explosions."

"I knew that boy was trouble," Elder Klosik muttered. "Go with Elder Mosley. Find Mr. Rudin and bring him in for questioning."

Elder Forese nodded. "Yes, sir."

Elder Mosley, a younger man with a strong build, jumped to his feet and followed Elder Forese out of the room.

Elder Klosik sat back in his chair, addressing the other two Elders, a middle aged woman and a younger man. "Elder Sanell, Elder Ryman, you've both been quiet."

The two exchanged glances, each waiting for the other to speak.

"Vara Sims was seen in the area as well, sir," Elder Sanell, the middle-aged woman, said with clear reluctance. "Two of my guards saw her."

Elder Klosik gave her a harsh sideways glance. "I think you should consider the strength of your case before proceeding any further."

"With all due respect and with Elder Ryman as my witness, I believe you're giving Vara preferential treatment because she is your daughter," Elder Sanell said. "Or should we call her your neice?"

"Your opinion is noted," Elder Klosik said with an

annoyed curl to his lip. "I'll put a surveillance team in her area. Now, if you'll excuse me, I have a new set of Holy Tablets to dictate."

Chapter III
THE PRODIGAL SON

"I don't know what you're talking about," Adtom said, his voice calm and even.

Raffi, his stepfather, paced the room, unable to hold still. "I'm not the only one who saw you! It's all over town!"

Adtom was a handsome young man with commanding blue eyes and sleek black hair. He had a strong build, far different from that of his frail, weak stepfather. Both men wore threadbare shirts and torn work pants, their garments scarred from years of abuse and repair.

The Rudins had a small workshop behind their house, where they crafted wooden furniture for townspeople and Elders alike. Raffi worked mostly on whittling and finishing, leaving the more laborous cutting and piecing to Adtom. The business continuously threatened to fail, mainly due to Adtom's defective work ethic, and the two experienced regular poverty as a result.

Adtom rolled his eyes at Raffi and let out a sigh. He replayed the event in his mind, positive that no one had seen him nor that anyone had followed him to the Worship Hall courtyard. He had ingeniously distracted the guards with a nearby explosion, a giant stone behind the Worship Hall that he had instantaneously reduced to shrapnel with a simple touch. Getting through the heavy gate to the Holy Tablets entailed another tap of the finger, and he was in before the guards had time to respond to his decoy.

The Holy Tablets stood upright, planted in the soft soil like gravestones at a cemetery. They were fashioned out of marble, the words of the Elders' god etched in deep, bold letters. Ten tablets in all, they were uniform in size, roughly shoulder-height to Adtom, and had been polished to perfection on all visible surfaces. He laid waste to every flawless detail, reducing the tablets, one by one, to dust. The act took much out of him, however, forcing him to retreat quickly with the little energy he had left.

Raffi finally broke the silence between them, both anger and fear in his voice as he yelled, "Don't you care at all about what you have done?"

There was a knock at the front door and Adtom turned to get it.

"Dear God, it's probably the Elders' guards!" Raffi cried, watching helplessly as Adtom reached the door and paused.

Raffi jumped as there was another even harder knock. "Adtom!" he called out as the young man flung open the door.

A lovely young woman stood on the front porch. "You said you were going to meet me by the lake!" she said, crossing her arms with a frown.

"I'm sorry, sweetheart. Something came up,"

Adtom said.

"We're not finished!" Raffi yelled from the living room.

Adtom ignored him. "Let me make it up to you," he said to the young woman. "I'll make you dinner tonight. How about that?"

The young woman shrugged. "What will you be making?"

"Adtom!" Raffi yelled even louder.

"Whatever you want." Adtom beamed his charming, superficial smile, giving the young woman a wink.

"Okay," she said, trying to sound reluctant.

"I'm a little busy right now, though, so if you wouldn't mind excusing me?"

"Oh, okay."

Adtom reached out and gave the young woman a peck on the cheek. "See you tonight." He closed the door and turned to Raffi.

"Who was that?" Raffi asked.

Adtom grinned. "A nice, tight virgin that's in desperate need of some loosening up."

The old man ran his hands through his thinning gray hair. "That's no way to treat a nice girl."

"She won't be so nice once I'm finished with her," Adtom said with a chuckle.

Raffi shook his head, turning away, and then he turned back for another moment, unable to resist asking any longer: "Why did you do it? Why did you destroy the Holy Tablets?"

Adtom gave a thoughtful sigh. "The Elders are liars and thieves, and it's time someone put them in their place."

Raffi looked down, shaking his head with disgust.

"What, no snide retort? You're not going to remind me what a horrible son I am?" Adtom asked. "Why don't you tell me again how wicked I must be to have killed my mother during childbirth?"

Raffi quietly continued to shake his head.

"Say *something*!" Adtom yelled, unnerved by Raffi's silence.

Raffi turned, glaring hatefully at Adtom. He began to shake, fighting tears. Finally, he said, "I know what you are!"

"What is that supposed to mean?"

"You don't have to play stupid with me! Not anymore!" Raffi cried.

Adtom charged Raffi, moving in uncomfortably close. "What the hell are you talking about?"

"You're not my son! You never were!"

Adtom grimaced, unable to hide the sting. "Why would you say something like that?"

Raffi cowered, silent once more.

"Tell me why you said it!" Adtom yelled.

Raffi fell to his knees as tears streamed down his face. "God, forgive me!"

Adtom shook the man. "Why would you say that?"

"Because it's the truth!" Raffi cried. "Sinda was a virgin! We saved your lives because we *believed* the prophecy!" Raffi covered his tear-soaked face. "We thought you were gods, but the Elders were right!"

"Oh really?" Adtom asked, suddenly indignant. "How were the Elders right?"

"You're the seed of the devil!" Raffi cried.

Adtom backed away from the man, the frail, old

man whom Adtom knew, now more than ever, was indeed not his father. He had suspected it for years, something deep within him telling him that he was different. Still, Raffi's words induced in him a sick, painful feeling, as if a dagger had found his stomach and now slowly tore through the core of his body.

"I have to go." Raffi got to his unsteady feet, his hands shaking violently.

"Where are you going?"

Raffi continued toward the door, ignoring the question.

Adtom hurried to pass him, then cut him off and blocked the door with his body.

"Get out of my way!" Raffi yelled.

"You're going to report me to the Elders, aren't you? Have me arrested and burned alive, is that it?"

"Why would you say that?" Raffi asked.

"A gut feeling, I guess."

"What, are you a mind-reader, too?" Raffi looked Adtom in the eyes, taking a deep breath.

Adtom stepped to the side of the door. "Go, have your only son sacrificed—sentenced to a horrific death—if that's what you think you need to do!"

Raffi stood, suddenly terrified to move, staring helplessly at the doorknob. He jumped as there was another knock at the door.

Adtom pushed Raffi aside and answered it, only allowing the door open a crack.

A different young woman stood on the front porch. "Hi, Adtom!"

Adtom smiled. "How have you been, baby?"

"Fine. I was wondering if you were free this afternoon."

Raffi tried to dart off, but Adtom excused himself for a moment to grab Raffi by the shirt collar. He dragged Raffi alongside him as he returned to the door and held the man behind it, just out of the young woman's sight. He flashed another smile at the girl as he hid the struggle behind the door. "I'm really busy tonight sweetie, but I'll make it up to you with a really nice dinner tomorrow night. How about that?"

The young woman smiled. "Okay."

Raffi began to writhe out of his shirt, loosening Adtom's hold of him. Adtom kept a calm, pleasant face for the young woman. "Listen, I'm kind of busy right now. I'll see you tomorrow evening?"

"Help!" Raffi cried weakly from behind the door.

Adtom cocked his head, playfully rolling his eyes. "I've got to go help my dad."

"Please!" Raffi continued.

"So, I'll see you tomorrow night?" Adtom asked the young woman with a confident wink.

She smiled back. "It's a date."

Adtom nodded, smiling sweetly, and then closed the door. He immediately threw Raffi to the floor. Raffi remained silent as for a moment as he and Adtom stared one another down.

"Where were we?" Adtom finally asked.

"Nowhere. Neither of us was doing anything!"

"Are you sure about that?"

Raffi stared up at him, unable to respond.

Adtom stood over the timid little man, daring him to get up.

"Please, you have to stop this!" Raffi cried.

Adtom opened the front door and took several steps away from it. He glared angrily, daring him to leave. "What are you waiting for?" He forced the man to his feet. "Stop me! Have your only son sentenced to death!"

Raffi began to bawl. He closed the door and gave Adtom a heartfelt hug. "Did you think I would ever be able to go through with it?"

Adtom smiled back, accepting the hug. He held the man tightly as he gave him a kiss on the head. "I *know* that you mean to go through with it, behind my back, at the next possible opportunity."

Raffi tried to break away from Adtom's hold, but his feeble limbs were no match for Raffi's strong grip. He could see in Adtom's eyes that something horrible was about to happen, and a gasp escaped him as Adtom suddenly gave a content smile. He fought harder, the young man's eyes suddenly cold and still. "What are you doing? Let me go, son!"

"I have a little secret," Adtom began, his voice lowering to a whisper. "I am death."

Raffi's eyes went wide as his heart stopped. He gasped, unable to breathe.

Adtom released his hold, allowing Raffi to slip to the ground. Raffi looked up at him, his eyes begging an appeal for his life. He reached up with one arm, fighting to muster up the breath for one desperate plea. His lips tried to move, but no words came forth.

"I've known for a long time," Adtom said as the body before him went lifeless. "All it takes is one touch."

Adtom stared at the body. Its eyes were much duller than they had been a moment ago, and yet they still stared up at him with the same emotion they'd shown while in life. Adtom had never killed a human being before, and it brought about sensations that were much different than those he found with the death of small animals or plants. It was also exhausting.

Just like the creatures he had experimented with in the past, there was no bringing this human being, the man he had thought for over thirty years to be his father, back from death. He was gone. Adtom considered the permanence of what he had done as he dragged the body to the nearest corner of the room, and he decided that it had been a necessary deed.

He grinned.

He opened the front door and stepped out onto the porch. He took a deep breath, contemplating what he should do next. There were people coming for him. They were on their way right now, their hearts set on his demise.

He just had a gut feeling.

Chapter IV
TRUTH OR DARE

Vara Sims sat in her lush, overgrown back yard. Several different types of vibrant flowers bloomed, and colorful birds and insects filled the air. Small animals scurried throughout the yard, disregarding any possible threat posed by Vara's presence.

Vara was a lovely woman with long, wildly curly hair and bright green eyes. Having been raised by the Elder and Mrs. Klosik, Vara had a firm respect for both faith and rules. Mrs. Klosik had an especially strong impact on Vara's upbringing, teaching Vara by example to be kind and generous. Vara was outgoing, remarkably empathetic, and, regarding her husband of two years, a hopeless romantic. She had an innate love of nature, and for reasons unbeknownst to her, animals of all kinds became tame to her when she was alone. She felt drawn to them too, with a desire to nurture and feed them. They were like the beautiful children she and her husband Ched still failed to have—and she did not mourn her difficulties in conceiving as he did. She kept the animals a secret, even from him, as much as she would have loved to have helped him fill his void by sharing them. It had to be that way.

She felt ashamed about it sometimes. Any good follower of the One True God understood that animals and plants did not have souls. Sometimes she would allow that notion to fix itself in the forefront of her mind, and for some reason the thought always sent her into fits of tears. They all loved her back, all of them. She knew that. She could feel it. She could feel *them*. How could something possibly be capable of love if it did not have a soul?

She shared her special relationship with no one. She would be deemed either a heathen or insane, as only demons conversed with birds and flowers, not to mention bugs and scavengers. She knew in her heart that she couldn't possibly be a demon, but also knew that there would be no convincing anyone else of that.

Carrying a small pouch filled with nuts and seeds, she had become engulfed in a game of hide-and-seek with a small group of animals. The game was simple: she took a treat from the pouch and tried to confuse them as to which hand she held the treat in. If one or more of the animals picked the correct hand, everyone got a treat.

She picked a nut from the pouch and juggled it between her hands. No one had correctly guessed her last two hands, so she decided to make this one easy. She held out both of her hands. "Okay, which one?"

A number of small animals and two of the larger birds guessed correctly, and Vara handed out a number of various nuts and seeds. "That one was too *easy*."

A baby bird nested in the tree above her eagerly watched as she started a new game. In its excitement, it lost its footing and toppled onto a large, flat rock. Vara hurried to it as its body convulsed, the life slipping from its tiny body. She knelt at its side.

The mother bird desperately circled overhead, screeching madly.

Vara took the tiny, limp creature into her hands, fighting tears. "No, you're . . . alive," she said. As she finished her words, the fledgling jumped to life and rolled to its feet. Vara smiled. "I thought so." She reached for the nest and returned the bird, and the frantic mother hurried to her nest with a disciplinary shriek.

Vara stepped back, watching the birds, then froze as the animals scattered. She turned, spotting the trespasser walking into the yard.

Vara jumped to her feet. "Hey! No one said you could come back here!"

The woman admired the lavish yard. Lush vines with bright, colorful flowers grew up the sides of the house. Bushes and trees, covered with flowers and laden with fruit, towered over the foliage from all of the neighboring properties.

"I knocked on the front door, but no one answered. My name is Jeza Khess. It's good to formally meet you," she said with a smile.

"Can I help you?" Vara asked, moving toward her back door.

"I know that we've never really talked in town, but I was wondering if I might have a moment of your time."

Vara nodded hesitantly. "Please come inside."

She led Jeza into the house.

She made a fresh pot of tea, offering her guest a seat in the living room. Jeza took in the humble but tasteful décor, making herself comfortable. She noticed the numerous clocks on the walls, their carved wooden frames each unique yet flawless, their arms set in identical precision, their pendulums swinging in perfect unison.

"Is your husband also available?"

"He's in his workshop. I can see if he can spare a minute."

Jeza nodded. "If you could."

Vara left, momentarily returning with her husband, Ched.

Ched was a nice-looking man with a thin build. He wore thick glasses and was dressed in oily coveralls. He owned the clock shop, working endless hours making and repairing clocks of all shapes and sizes.

"Ms. Khess?" Ched shook Jeza's hand. "What can we do for you?"

She took a moment to compose her words. Finally, she cleared her throat and began to speak: "The destruction of the Holy Tablets has put the Elders on high alert—"

"I'm sorry, but just because Elder Klosik is my father, that doesn't mean I have any weight on his decisions. If you have any thoughts on the Tablets, you really need to talk to someone who works for the Eldership," Vara interrupted.

"I need you both to just take a moment and hear me out. What I'm about to say might sound a bit wild, but—"

Ched rolled his eyes. "She's a salesperson! Wasting my precious time!" Ched stood to leave.

"No, wait! I just want to talk!"

Ched stood at the door. "I'm very busy on a project right now, so if you could get to whatever you need to say as quickly as possible I'd really appreciate it."

"You're two of the five in the prophecy—" Jeza began, suddenly feeling desperate to hold their attention.

"You've got to be kidding me!" Vara stood, outraged. "You know who my father is!"

"Elder Klosik is not your father."

"You come into my house to say such horrible and outlandish things?" Vara asked. "Who the hell do you think you are?"

"You are both in danger. I need you to pack what you can carry and come with me," Jeza continued.

"Listen, I don't know why you've chosen us specifically to do this to, but I'm going to have to ask you to leave!" Ched said, his voice angry and stern. "You've upset my wife."

"I'm sorry. I didn't mean to." Jeza stayed where she was. "Please, I need you to listen to me. Give me just a couple minutes of your time."

Ched charged toward her. "Get out!"

"There's something different about you, both of you." Jeza knew the answer but she had to ask, just the same: "Neither of you can so much as feel it?"

Neither responded.

"Adtom Rudin shattered the Holy Tablets last night," Jeza continued. "There was more than one witness." Jeza glanced at Vara, who feigned ignorance.

"So the Elders will have him arrested, and we all get to watch him burn. What is your point?" Ched asked, taking a quick, dramatic look up at one of the clocks.

"Adtom shattered the Tablets with a mere touch of his fingers. Word is spreading through town that he is a demon." Jeza looked Vara straight in the eyes, her face sincere. "He killed his stepfather this morning. I *know* you felt that."

Ched pointed to one of the clocks. "We've got things to do. Nice chatting with you, really, but it's time for you to go now." Ched pulled Jeza from her seat and began to escort her to the front door.

Jeza resisted, speaking quickly. "You built your first clock when you were five. You would have built one earlier, but your parents hadn't allowed you access to the parts you needed."

Ched released his grip on Jeza's arm. "How do you know that?"

"When your parents died in that carriage accident, you felt as though time stopped for just a—"

"You leave my parents out of this!" Ched snapped.

Jeza took a deep, weary breath, then continued, "You met Vara at the Elder picnic, and you thought to yourself that you had never before seen a woman with so much life in her eyes. You wanted to go to her and introduce yourself, but you were afraid she would reject you. You were pleasantly surprised when she came to you, just as shy, and introduced herself to you."

Ched backed away from Jeza, staring her down. "I never told anyone that."

"I know." She turned to Vara. "You're terrified of Elder Klosik . . . because, deep down, you know you're no safer from him than anyone else."

Vara hurried to Ched's side, fighting tears. "What do you *want* from us?"

"I just need you to trust me for now."

Ched shook his head, speaking for them both. "I don't think so."

"We came to bring peace to the people, so we could learn from them, but when we got here we lost our way," Jeza said. "I'm the only one who remembers everything from the beginning. I'm the only one who knows who Adtom Rudin—who each of us—really is."

"You're crazy!" Vara cried out.

"Worse than that, I'm afraid," Ched muttered. In a long, exaggerated step, he bravely moved between Jeza and his wife, staring Jeza down. "Leave now, demon! You are not welcome in any home of the One True God's believers!"

"I'm a demon, then?" Jeza asked, the collective wisdom of the universe insufficient enough to provide her with any better response.

The unbodied consciousness had made a mistake, Jeza thought, fighting tears. Perhaps, in taking such a radical approach in choosing to separate for the sake of their human bodies, God may have corrupted and ruined the original, creative whole forever. What if they were now lost, permanently distorted by what they had made of themselves?

"I don't know what else to say," Jeza said, bowing her head in apology. "We made this choice, and now I suppose we have to live with it." She left the house, terrified and disheartened. As she walked down the dirt path, she thought to go home, and then decided to try Len Telan despite her discouragement.

She passed a small group of young children playing in an open field off the side of the road. The children ran and giggled, hitting a small ball back and forth with large sticks. Jeza smiled. Virtue still existed in the world, even if only in the hearts of its children. There was still hope.

After walking for some time, she turned down the path leading to the Telan house and hurried off the open road.

Len was a chemist and physicist, and the only scientist in documented history to have successfully demonstrated the ability to practice alchemy. Fine metals of his own creation adorned his house, his wealth second only to that of the Elders—to whom he was notoriously generous.

Jeza knocked on Len's front door. The large house was intimidating, as if it had a life of its own. Although Jeza knew to the contrary, it seemed as if it had started out as a small house and, somehow at Len's bidding, grew into the enormous structure that now stood before her.

Finely carved statuettes of different metals and gems adorned the front porch. The outside walls had small jewels embedded in them, which created small mosaics of different colorful shapes across the face of the entire stone and wooden structure. Jeza knocked again, but no one answered.

She looked into her mind's eye, finding Len working in his lab. He held a small, dull stone in one hand. In the other, he had a dropper filled with an opaque indigo liquid. He carefully dispersed the liquid onto the stone, one drop, then another. His hand began to shake as the stone slowly grew heavier, a bright golden sheen developing across its surface. He took a deep breath, setting down the stone to admire his work. He turned to the door as Jeza banged once again on the hard wood. With an impatient sigh, he stood from his chair, ascended the staircase, and exited his workshop.

Jeza watched intently as the door cracked open.

"May I help you?" Len asked, peeking through the crack.

"Len Telan, my name is Jeza Khess. I know you don't remember me, but we've done business before in the town square."

"I'm not interested in buying anything."

Jeza rolled her eyes. "I don't have anything to sell!"

Hesitant, Len opened the door just enough for the two to view one another face to face.

Len was a short, thin young man with dark shaggy hair and onyx eyes. He scowled at Jeza. "What do you want, then?"

"I was wondering if I could have a moment of your time," Jeza replied.

"I'm really busy," Len said, and moved to close the door.

Jeza blocked the door with her foot. "Everybody's busy! A minute is all I ask. I need to speak with Lanora."

Len's mother had suffered ill health for years, from a disease that slowly consumed her lungs and wasted her body to a mere skeleton. She rarely left

43

her bed for any length of time these days, spending the majority of her time counting the endless hours, writhing and moaning in her agony. She refused to see anyone shortly after she had become an invalid, not wanting her friends to watch her die, and those friends, who all cared deeply for her, had no choice but to leave the Telans be and wait for word that Lanora had finally passed.

"I'm sorry, but she'll see no one."

"She'll see me."

"I assure you that she won't." Len tried to close the door, but Jeza blocked it with her leg.

"Just go and ask her! Tell her Jeza Khess is here to see her!"

"Wait here." Len pushed Jeza through the door and closed it. As Jeza waited for him to return, she marveled again at the amazing metalwork that adorned the house and yard. It had taken Len years to fashion all of the small masterpieces that now clung to the building, covered the porch, and even sprung from the earth. It was no surprise that the Elders held him in such high favor.

Len opened the door, looking surprised. "Please come in."

Len led Jeza into a cool, sterile room. Lanora lay in her bed, with clean white sheets covering her thin, dying body. Len stood in the threshold as Jeza walked up to the bed.

Lanora knew Jeza as soon she walked into the room, even though they had not crossed paths since Jeza was a child. Lanora smiled, and yet her face still showed nothing but pain. "Jeza? Jeza Khess, is that really you?"

"It's me," Jeza said, taking the woman's hand. "It's been a long time."

"Yes, it has."

"I need you to do me a favor," Jeza said.

"Yes?"

"I need you to tell your son the truth."

"The truth?" Lanora asked.

Jeza nodded. "About everything."

Lanora's face went blank. "You know? But Avani was never supposed to say anything—"

"She never did."

"So how did you find out?" Lanora began to cough, choking for a moment. She rocked forward, catching her breath, then collapsed back against her pillow.

"I've always known."

Lanora took a strained breath. "I see."

"What?" Len asked, lost in the conversation.

"We didn't mean to come the way we did. We thought things would be different." Jeza sat down beside Lanora. "Please, if we have any chance, I need for the others to know—and I'm sure Len won't believe me if I try to tell him, myself." She glanced over at Len.

"What am I supposed to say?" Lanora asked.

"Whatever it takes."

Lanora nodded. "I'll do my best."

Jeza gave Lanora a kiss on the forehead, and then walked to the door. "I'll be in touch."

"What's going on?" Len asked.

"I'm trying a different approach," Jeza said. "I'll show myself out now. The two of you have a lot to discuss."

Jeza walked down the road, turning onto the main street. Len would listen to Lanora. Of course, she still needed to find some way to get through to Vara and Ched, which would be a difficult task. She thought about the others as she made her way down the long stretch of road. As she walked, with nothing but her thoughts to accompany her for the couple of miles ahead, she wondered what it would take to convince Vara and Ched of the truth. Both had been even more resistant than she had anticipated. For their strengths, each had a weakness for the people's myths. Then there was Adtom, who had incidentally just found himself in a great deal of trouble. . . .

Distraught, Jeza hurried into town. She passed a number of peddlers who fled down the path with their loaded carts from the town square. "Turn around!" one of them warned her. "If you value your life, turn around and run!"

Adtom stood in the heart of the town square. Five corpses lay surrounding the man, their weapons scattered. He sweated profusely, eyeing the mob of people around him like a caged beast. The people kept their distance, the Elders huddling together within the mob, trying to decide what to do.

"Who wants to die next?" Adtom cried. He turned to the Elders. "I'll take on the lot of you! Arm yourselves with whatever you'd like. Let's see how well your god truly protects his believers!"

Elder Klosik turned to Elder Ryman. "We can't have this! Take him down!"

"But Elder—"

"God will protect the faithful!"

Terrified and hesitant, yet with a growing look of

resolve etched across his face, Elder Ryman picked up a sword from the ground and charged toward Atdom. He raised the sword over his head, knowing that he had no choice but to kill or be killed. "Surrender now—in the name of God!" he yelled, his voice quavering.

"Stand down now or die—in the name of the devil!" Adtom replied, and then spat on the Elder's shoes.

"God, protect me!" Elder Ryman cried as he brought down the blade, trying to catch Adtom before his focus shifted from the insulting act.

Adtom pivoted, shoving Elder Ryman away from him before his blade could hit its mark, and watched him collapse to the ground, lifeless.

Silence.

A sudden roar of screams and wails filled the square.

Adtom staggered, visibly weakening. He wiped the sweat from his face as he looked around for any further contenders.

Jeza ran up to the horrified crowd and pushed her way into the center. Adtom had just murdered six people, one of them an Elder, yet she sensed from him nothing but pride.

"Adtom! Stop this!" Jeza cried.

Adtom turned to her. "Try to make me. I dare you!"

Jeza kept her distance, knowing that her body was just as susceptible to injury or death as any other standing in the square. What she did not know was what would become of her if she were to part from this world without the four others.

She held up her hands to show that she was not armed. "I know you're scared—"

"I'm not scared!"

"—but I just want to talk," she said.

"Back off!" he yelled.

Jeza began to inch her way toward Adtom. "You can trust me. We're allies, you and I. I just want to help."

"Stay where you are!" Adtom commanded.

Jeza continued, her movements slow. "I'm an unarmed woman. Are you going to murder me in cold blood?"

"Test me!" he yelled.

Jeza stopped, now just within arm's reach of him. "Don't be afraid," she said, putting her hand on his shoulder.

Adtom collapsed, unconscious.

The crowd let out a united gasp.

Jeza gently lifted Adtom into her arms, struggling with the limp weight, and began to stagger toward the edge of the circle. "Out of my way!" she yelled ahead of her.

The crowd abided, the people keeping their distance as Jeza carried Adtom out of the circle and away from the town square. As she parted, the terrified group swarmed over their deceased Elder, studying the body, too afraid to touch it.

Elder Klosik watched Jeza drag Adtom into the distance. He turned to address his people, holding his arms to his back to hide his trembling hands. "The enemy has revealed itself, but we are stronger. She retreats because she knows the power of the One True God. Let us pray."

Jeza commandeered a cart just down the path, watching the townspeople in her mind's eye for any followers. She heaved the limp body into the cart and wheeled it home.

To her relief, no one dared to follow her.

Chapter V
THE DEAD LANDS

Jeza and Avani took their time setting up camp. They worked together to assemble a large tent, hammering stakes into the ground and pulling the material taut.

The Dead Lands stretched for miles all around them. The ground was sandy and dark, most of it loose and flat. The sand had formed dunes in some areas where it was especially windy, and the dark, rocky remnants of mountains lay across one horizon. Beyond the wind, which was relatively calm in the area Jeza chose for camp, there was nothing but silence.

Adtom slept peacefully, lying benignly on a lightweight but steady cot until they were ready to deal with him. Jeza and Avani had brought him by cart, along with as many supplies as they could manage, and the slow journey had taken much out of both of them. The tent they had set up for Adtom was small and the air inside, even with the flaps open, was hot and humid. He lay in a thin film of his own sweat, silent and still.

Jeza and Avani finished pitching the second, larger tent for themselves, and then sat in the shade of the roughly six-foot square structure. A small pile of wood lay between the two tents, beside four lightweight jugs of water. Avani grabbed one of the jugs and took a sip, then offered it to Jeza.

Jeza accepted the jug, and also took a small sip from it. "Thanks. I needed that."

"I had forgotten how hot it gets out here."

Jeza nodded in agreement as she got to her feet and went over to the three remaining jugs of water. She dug a shallow hole, and then buried one of the jugs. With Avani's help, Jeza buried the remaining jugs in separate holes within close proximity of one another. They scattered the sand to disguise the disturbed land.

Jeza walked over to the smaller tent, carrying the remaining water jug, kneeling back down to enter. She set down the jug of water and went to Adtom's side.

She wiped some of the sweat from his forehead. He looked peaceful, so different from the monster she had dragged from the town square. She watched him for a moment, studying his face, working up the courage to revive him.

"Time to wake," she said softly, then backed to the edge of the tent as Adtom stirred.

He sat up quickly. Jeza could feel his confused thoughts as he struggled to process the situation. The last thing he remembered was standing in the town square and Jeza boldly approaching him. She sensed his alarm and confusion.

"What happened? Where am I?" he asked.

"You're safe," Jeza said.

"You were in the town square." Adtom wiped his sweaty face, and then ran his fingers through his warm, damp hair. He was ready to run if he needed to. "How did I get here?"

"I brought you here."

He shook his head, dizzy from the heat. "But how? We were surrounded."

She shrugged. "How did you destroy the Elders' stone tablets and kill all of those people?"

A sudden look of desperation filled his eyes. "You're a devil too?"

"We're not devils." She lifted a jug of water from her side and offered it to him.

He stared hesitantly.

"It's not drugged," she said, sensing his thoughts. Realizing that his paranoia would not easily abate, she took a sip and swallowed it with a heavy gulp. Again, she extended it to him.

He snatched the jug from her hands and began to drink.

"Try to ration yourself. We need to make it last."

Jeza's tension began to wane as she recognized Adtom's relief. She knew well enough not to trust him, but at the same time she felt the kinship between the two of them. She wanted to comfort him, teach him what she knew, and offer him some direction.

He set down the jug and wiped his face. "You didn't answer my question. Where am I?"

"We've set up camp a day's walk into the Dead Lands."

"I don't understand."

"Let's get out of this hot tent. There's nice breeze

passing through right now." Jeza left, motioning for Adtom to follow.

Reluctantly, Adtom followed her out.

Jeza and Adtom met Avani in the shade of the larger tent.

Jeza motioned to Avani. "This my mother."

Adtom gave the woman a customary nod.

"She was one of the five prophesied virgins."

Adtom shook his head adamantly. "The virgins all died at the stake."

"All five of us lived," Avani corrected. "We lived here for months, our families all covering for our whereabouts, bringing us supplies. Four of us returned with child." Avani looked at Adtom remorsefully. "We buried your mother somewhere out here. She was a good woman and a dear friend."

Adtom gave her an annoyed glance. "You don't know me very well if you think I was chosen by God to do anything here."

"You were chosen by no one. *We* all chose this," Jeza said.

"Why would we do that?"

"We thought we could set up a framework for peaceful existence here, and in the process also learn something important from the people," Jeza said.

"I'm sorry, but that's the lamest story I've ever heard." He gave an exaggerated laugh. He didn't believe in the Elder's obviously fabricated deity, and he certainly wasn't about to entertain the idea that God, if there was one, could learn something from the *people*. "You must be heathens. My father always said that heathens had pathetic gods!"

Jeza and Avani exchanged glances.

"I'm blessed to have gotten the wise one," Avani mused.

Jeza smiled.

"You're saying I'm a god?" Adtom asked, just to hear himself say the words. He laughed, this time for real. He pointed to Jeza. "And you're a god, too?"

"In a sense, I like to think of us more as prophets, but 'god' works just as well, I guess."

"Then why aren't all of us omnipresent and all-powerful? Isn't God omnipresent and all-powerful?"

"That's just not how we chose to be."

Adtom laughed even harder. "Unbelievable! I'm lost in the Dead Lands, with two complete lunatics as my company! Women lunatics at that! We have enough water for, what, a day? What luck!" Adtom's laughter waned, and his mood suddenly became very serious. "Which way leads to town?" His eyes pierced through Jeza. "Do you know?"

"Town is northwest," she said.

"I want your compass."

"We didn't bring a compass," she said, her patience wearing thin, frustrated by the lack of cooperation she had so far received from the others.

"Then how do you know which way is northwest?" he asked, looking around in a sudden panic. "Are we specifically southeast, or is that just your closest guess? How are we going to get back to town?"

"I know *everything*, that's how!" Jeza snapped. She stared at Adtom, fuming. She was fully aware that she did not know everything, per se, but the human part of her made her scream it out anyway. She felt guilty for having said it. Even as the unbodied consciousness, God had unanswered questions—countless unanswered questions. She took a moment to compose herself, to remember the larger scheme.

"Calm down. He doesn't know any better," Avani said, placing a hand on Jeza's shoulder.

"I'm sorry," Jeza said, shaking her head. "We had no idea it would turn out like this. I'm just about at my wit's end."

"Which way is northwest?" Adtom demanded.

"Why would you want to go back to town?" Jeza asked.

"Does it matter? You can't make me stay here!"

"If you go back right now, you'll only find yourself up against more attacks. Is that what you want?"

"Let them attack. I'll just—"

"Kill them all?" Jeza finished for him, disgusted. "That's not what you came here to do." She turned away, angered by Adtom's hard head and hefty ego.

"So what do you propose?"

Jeza had a feeling that the five of them would need to work together if they were going to salvage anything out of the experience. Beyond that, she felt about as ill-equipped as the rest of them. "It'll come to me."

Adtom rolled his eyes. "You're out of your mind!"

Ignoring him, Jeza went to the mouth of the large tent and began to dig around for a small snack. Adtom's continued racing thoughts disturbed her, and she had to remind herself that death and destruction were not evil; they were part of the natural laws that came with the existence of matter. Still, Adtom came across even to Jeza as more of a demon than a part of God. She wondered, in hindsight, why the unbodied consciousness had allowed its characteristics to divide so randomly among the five prophets. It had not meant to unleash such a monster upon the people.

Jeza sighed. She could not allow herself to think of him in such simple terms. Adtom was not a monster, and she of all people knew better than to divide the values of gods and devils.

Avani smiled. "Have faith, Adtom. Jeza is a very wise woman."

"Faith is something I lost a long time ago, lady."

"That's too bad." Avani reached for a pouch and grabbed a handful of dice. She began to roll them, watching the random results. "Faith is something everybody should have."

"Faith in what? In the Holy Tablets? The lost Holy Books?"

"Faith in something." Avani cleared the sand in front of her to create a proper rolling surface.

Jeza passed out sticks of dried meat and returned to her spot beside Avani.

Adtom was hesitant, watching the two women eat for a moment as he evaluated his serving.

"The meat's not drugged or poisoned either. Take it or leave it," Jeza said.

Adtom took a piece of meat, and the three began to chew at their food.

Adtom watched Avani roll her dice as she ate.

"What made you lose your faith?" Avani asked him.

Adtom shrugged. "Does it matter?"

"Of course it matters." Avani sat back and waited for Adtom to ask:

"Why?"

Avani rolled the dice a few more times, until she got a combination with heavy odds against it. "Because life is random. Unexpected things happen, and our lives often play out very differently than we might imagine."

"So?"

"So, if you don't allow yourself to believe in something, more than just a series of random events, then you've reduced your life to nothing more than a game of dice." Avani picked up the dice and handed them to Adtom.

"A game of dice is all it is, regardless of what you choose to believe in." Adtom closed the dice in his hand, then opened it, revealing nothing left but dust. He allowed the dust to blow from his hand, and then wiped the remnants off on his shirt. "You claim that faith gives hope, faith heals . . . right? I say faith kills, faith destroys, and faith crushes hopes. I say faith is an excuse, a means to divert personal blame. I say faith is for the weak . . . the weak of mind, and the weak of heart."

Jeza considered Adtom's words and the dark thoughts that came along with them, knowing that he was not altogether wrong in his assessment. Still, she felt a strong urge to tell him otherwise. It was not faith that destroyed lives, but faith misplaced. The world would not be any better place without it, and yet she had to wonder if it would be any worse for its absence. She studied Adtom's angry face and opted to finish eating her ration in silence.

Chapter VI
THE ELDER'S LEGACY

Elder Klosik invited Vara and Ched Sims over for dinner, stating that Lauru insisted the two eat properly every once in a while. Although Vara's humility told her that she and Ched should eat the same way the rest of the common people did, Ched would never allow her to decline an invitation to a good meal.

The food was lavish. Lauru had roasted game fowl, and offered sides of different colorful fruits and vegetables in large, crystalline bowls. The servants offered them warm, sweet breads, and poured glasses of fresh, cool water and juice. The Elder and Lauru drank hard cider, which was available exclusively to the Elders.

Ched filled his plate with a sample of everything offered. He ate quickly, the array of expensive and exquisite foods too tempting to pass up, while Vara, pacing herself, felt thoroughly embarrassed by her husband's lack of self-control.

"Thank you so much for inviting us, sir," she said to Elder Klosik, speaking as any other common person would to the man. She worked hard to achieve eye contact with him, and when she finally did, she immediately turned back to her plate. "This is far more than any clockmaker's family deserves. You are too generous."

Elder Klosik nodded, almost producing a smile. He had been duly militant in his approach to Vara's upbringing, and as a result he had molded a fine servant of the Eldership. She had a healthy fear of authority and a hearty respect for her Elders. "The Eldership is good to its people," he said, as if the response held some type of relevance to Vara's humble remark.

Ched held his tongue, opting to stuff his mouth rather than speak.

"I was delighted when your father said you'd come. I made all of your favorites," Lauru said, glad to have the company.

"It's all very good," Vara said.

Ched grunted with a nod, unable to speak through his food-filled mouth.

"I do have sort of an ulterior motive for the invite," Elder Klosik said with a sigh.

A chill ran down Vara's spine, and she held back a fearful cringe. She and Ched both gave Elder Klosik their full attention.

"My sources tell me that Jeza Khess was at your house yesterday," Elder Klosik said.

"Yes, she was," Vara said.

"I've also been told that you were seen near Adtom Rudin the night he destroyed the tablets," Elder Klosik continued, eyeing Vara.

"You don't think that I—" Vara began.

"Of course I don't," Elder Klosik interrupted. "I just want to know what you were doing when you were seen with those people."

"But I wasn't seen *with* Adtom—"

"But you were seen with Jeza Khess, and unfortunately right now that puts both of you under suspicion," Elder Klosik said, his face flat and unreadable.

"Is this an interrogation?" Ched asked, temporarily abandoning his meal.

The Elder smiled. "You would not be eating fine fruits and game fowl if this were an interrogation."

"It sure seems like one to me," Lauru muttered.

"Leave us!" Elder Klosik snapped, shooting her a sharp glare.

Lauru glared back, and their eyes tested one another for a short moment. She looked determined not to give in, not this time, and yet his eyes held on her, commanding and intimidating. Finally, she turned away in angry submission. She hurried out, biting her tongue and gritting her teeth.

As of late, Lauru lived in a surreal state of denial and complacency, turning her back to the inconsistencies between the Holy Tablets and the Elders' rules and teachings, convincing herself with great tact that her faith was steadfast and her privileged life was both satisfying and without compromise. In truth, the Elder had come to treat her as he would any of his other servants, save the fact that he allowed her the occasional glass or two of hard cider when her nerves got the better of her. He preferred the personal company of his concubines to their conjugal bed, and he favored the intellectual company of his peers to any quality time the two of them might share. Lauru's house was always bustling with servants, her every need tended to, yet her life had become empty, her days meaningless.

Now, the only person Lauru still felt any bond with was being considered a potential threat to the Eldership. She tried to convince herself that the whole mess would blow over soon enough, that no harm would come of the Elders' current inquiry. She also knew, however, that potential threats, no matter how imagined they may be, were always taken very seriously by the Elders.

"You're lucky that I have kept this a private matter up to this point," Elder Klosik said to Vara. "Now, if you want to keep things that way, I need to know your story."

Vara nodded, unable to keep from shaking. "Okay, I'll tell you. I have nothing to hide. I followed Adtom to the sacred vault because I just happened upon him. I thought he was acting suspiciously."

"Why didn't you report him?"

Vara shook her head. "I don't know. I was afraid."

"Afraid of what?"

Vara shrugged, and then decided to draw up a defense that the Elder was sure to sympathize with. "I was afraid of what he would do to me . . . he's obviously a demon. I was terrified."

Elder Klosik nodded. "And what about Jeza Khess?"

"That crazy freak," Ched muttered.

"What?" Elder Klosik asked, curious.

61

Vara and Ched looked at one another, neither looking able to find the right words. Vara's heart raced and her hands shook so badly that she had to hide them under the table.

"She came into our home uninvited and started rambling on about a bunch of nonsense," Ched finally said.

Vara nodded. "That's the best way to put it, definitely. Complete nonsense."

Elder Klosik eyed both Vara and Ched with suspicion. "What did she tell you?"

Vara hesitated, clearing her throat. "It was all just so ridiculous. I really don't—"

"What did she say?" the Elder demanded, his voice stern and his face serious.

"She said . . ." Vara paused, swallowing hard. Her throat went dry as she summoned the courage to force out the words: "She told me that you weren't my father."

"She said that?" Elder Klosik asked, suddenly looking uneasy.

Vara nodded. She looked over at Ched, and her desperate eyes met his.

"What else did she tell you?" Elder Klosik insisted.

Ched moved closer to Vara's side. "She told us that she was in league with Adtom Rudin and wanted us to join her. Of course, we banished her from our house."

"That's what happened," Vara agreed.

"How big is his group?" Elder Klosik asked.

"It's hard to tell," Ched said. "But it sounds like they're very organized."

"And Jeza is definitely one of their leaders," Vara quickly added, her hands fidgeting beneath the table.

"Would you be willing to repeat all of this under oath?" Elder Klosik asked.

Vara and Ched both nodded.

"I'm really sorry I didn't come to you earlier with this," Vara said. She cleared her throat, and she looked like she was on the verge of tears. "I should have. I was just really scared of what would happen to us. I promise I'll never withhold information from the Eldership again!"

Elder Klosik nodded, looking satisfied. "Now that that's settled." He called toward the kitchen. "Lauru, dear, we're just dying to try your cake!"

Lauru entered momentarily, bringing in an elaborately decorated cake. Her face was puffy with tears, but she smiled brightly and everyone else fell in line.

The evening continued as if nothing out of the ordinary had occurred, but no one who dined that night at the Klosiks' table slept well. Vara and Ched both lay in bed for most of the night, insomnia leaving them both tired and restless. Ched was able to get a small amount of sleep, although his rest was riddled with nightmares. He dreamt that he and Vara were trapped in their house, and that it was ablaze and filled with black, stifling smoke. They ran through the rooms as flames shot at them from all directions. The clocks on the walls burned and melted. One of them struck six and began to chime, but instead of chiming, it screamed and wailed as the flames slowly devoured it.

Ched cried out in his sleep, and Vara turned to

gently nudge him. "Ched—wake up!"

Ched jumped with a start and sat up. His body shook and his body glistened with sweat. He wiped his face and wrapped the blanket tightly around him.

"Are you okay?" Vara asked, knowing it had been another nightmare.

He nodded.

She wrapped her arms around him, warming his body with her own, urging him to lie back down with her.

She laid her body over his, resting her head on his chest, tucking the blanket around them both. She held him tight. "It was just a dream," she whispered.

Ched felt his body warm up next to hers. He kissed her on the forehead, then stared up at the dark ceiling.

Chapter VII
THE ELDERS' LEGACY

The next morning, Elder Klosik paced in his ready room, preparing for his service. He would be there for most of the day to research Elder Ryman's replacment officer, a young man named Cyrul Trevin. For now, he had the pressing issue of presenting the first of many sermons promoting the changes he and the other Elders had discovered when re-interpreting the Holy Tablets he had memorized.

The people waited patiently as Elder Klosik made his way to his podium, organizing his notes and gathering his nerves. "Good people, believers of the One True God," he finally began, "we, your trusted Elders, have worked endless hours to begin restoring the Tablets that were so viciously taken from us."

The people began to cheer.

Elder Klosik raised his hands to quiet the crowd. When silence finally fell upon the room, Elder Klosik continued: "We began with the Tablet of God's Holy Commandments, which now stands, safely locked away in an undisclosed place. As we restore the others, they too will be locked away, and their location will only be known by myself and the other four Elders. For those who need reminding of these commandments, I'm going to read them off to you right now."

Elder Klosik stared down at his notes, and read directly from them: "The Six Holy Commandments," he began with an authoritative voice. "Number one: 'There is only One True God. All nonbelievers shall be judged by their Elders.'" He surveyed his audience for a moment. All eyes were on him, eager and trusting.

"Number two: 'Any crime against the Eldership is a crime against God. Any persons believed to have committed a crime against God shall be judged by their Elders.'"

The people nodded, although a look of unease began to permeate the collective mask of contentment.

"Number three: 'Any persons found to have committed any crime against any of his or her fellow people shall be judged by their Elders.'"

Again, the people nodded.

"Number four: 'All whores, liars, blasphemers and perverts shall be judged by their Elders.'"

A few people cleared their throats and exchanged glances.

Elder Klosik pretended not to notice the sudden scrutiny. "Number five: 'All of the people shall pay a tithe to the Eldership. Any who refuse to pay a tithe, or fall into criminal debt to the Eldership, shall be judged by their Elders.'"

A light murmur filled the room.

Elder Klosik raised his voice. "Number six: 'All judgments made by the Elders are final.'"

The murmur grew to a small din.

Elder Klosik paused for a moment, watching the people. He made eye contact with as many individuals as he could, and slowly the room fell silent once more.

"The second Holy Tablet, that which governs the Elders' rule, also now lies perfectly restored beside the first. I have chosen today's sermon from that second Holy Tablet." He paused again, assessing the peoples' response, then continued: "The Tablet states that 'the wisdom of the One True God shall reside within the hearts and minds of the Elders, and they shall rule the people as His emissaries.' It is up to us, your Elders, to ensure that you all live, safe and happy, without fear of demons and terrorists wreaking havoc on our beautiful society. That has come at a cost, as much as we wish God could also provide the monetary means to keep the Eldership running; we have asked for your tithes, and you have all given faithfully."

A few people began to cheer, while others whispered speculations among their neighbors. Elder Klosik cleared his throat. He took a deep breath, his face going grave. He eyed every individual in the large room before he continued.

"We have ruled the people with fairness and justice. We have kept war from returning to the people, despite the demonic efforts," Elder Klosik said, his voice persuasively sincere. "And, as thankful as we are of your past generosity, we must ask that the people contribute even more now in our greatest hour of need." He paused, preparing himself for what he was about to say next.

"As you all know, there is a terrorist group of heathens working to destroy us. We were not able to save our original Holy Tablets in time, but we are determined to make sure that nothing like that ever happens again. We need to do everything possible to expose every person involved. It is our duty to ensure that all heathens and blasphemers burn to death, as commanded in the Holy Tablets. In order to do this, we have decided that we need full access to all of the people, as well as their property and correspondences, at all times."

The room became filled with a roar of commotion.

"It is only for your own protection that we have decided upon this. With your cooperation, the glory of the One True God will prevail!" Elder Klosik spoke over the peoples' furor. "We have already found one of them. Guards, bring him in!"

Two guards escorted a young man up to the Elders. He was bound by chains, and had to be dragged through the room.

"Let me go!" the young man screamed. "I didn't do anything!"

The guards tossed the young man to his knees, where he sat, staring up at Elder Klosik.

"By intimately observing the activities of the people, we found this man, Jode Sadin, to be conspiring against the Eldership with the heathen terrorists!" Elder Klosik proclaimed.

"You've got the wrong guy!" Jode cried. "I've been nothing but faithful!" He searched the room for a friendly face, but no one was willing to look him in the eyes.

Elder Klosik looked out upon the crowd. "Does anyone here wish to vouch for the faith of this man and try to prove his innocence—and share his fate, should he be found guilty?"

The crowd went still.

Again, Jode desperately searched the room. "Please! Somebody!"

Elder Klosik waited.

"I won't confess to something I didn't do!" Jode cried desperately.

"We don't need a confession," Elder Klosik informed him. "As the emissaries of God, we will judge you as we see fit."

Jode pled to the crowd: "You have to believe me! Those of you who know me *know* I wouldn't conspire with heathens! When was I supposedly seen? What was I supposedly doing? Tell me! Someone say *something*!"

Elder Sanell stood, addressing Jode with a hateful eye. "I saw you myself, trying to break into the back of the Worship Hall!" Elder Sanell glared at the people. "He had a bag filled with flammable materials on him. I caught him just before he was about to burn it down!"

The crowd roared in disgust.

"I was on my way home, on the paths, when the guards came out of nowhere and arrested me! I was bringing home a bottle of oil for the lamps, and that's all! I didn't do anything to deserve this!" Jode insisted. "You have to believe me!"

"Lies! We see how the devil turns the minds of

his minions deceitful and destructive!" Elder Klosik shouted with great passion in his voice.

"No, please!" Jode cried.

"Be silent, heathen!" Elder Sanell snapped.

The entire room went silent.

"Today, before the Eldership and all of its people, we your Elders judge you, Jode Sadin, guilty of committing crimes against the Eldership, and hereby sentence you to burn at the sacrificial stakes until dead, tomorrow at sunrise," Elder Klosik declared. "Guards, take this man back to his cell."

"But I'm innocent! Someone . . . please! You can't let them do this to me!" Jode's anguished cries echoed through the Worship Hall as the guards dragged him, kicking and screaming, out of the room.

Elder Klosik glanced over the silent crowd, assessing the individual reactions. "We now also know the identity of the heathen terrorist's leader is Jeza Khess. We are offering a reward of two months of free tithe to anyone directly aiding in the live capture of this woman or her associate, Adtom Rudin. To fund this reward, we will need to enforce a temporary ten percent increase on all of your tithes, beginning immediately."

A low hum of whispers filled the room, the people looking amongst one another for someone amongst them brave enough to speak up.

Elder Forese began to sing one of her favorite hymns, her eyes inviting the disgruntled people to join her. The people resisted, wanting somehow to express their disapproval of the tithe raise, but their resistance was short lived. The Elder sang of perseverence and trust, her song heartfelt and melodic. One by the one, the people joined in, reaffirming their faith in the Elders' wisdom . . . the emissaries of their One True God.

Elder Klosik watched as the collection plates started their rounds. "As always, we thank you for your cooperation."

Elder Klosik did a thorough background check on Cyrul Trevin that afternoon, finding the young man to have an exemplary past. Cyrul had completed all of his religious studies courses with passion, and had written a brilliant paper on Seer, the man whom God had led to the Holy Tablets. Taking three months to retrace the steps Seer took when he disappeared into the Dead Lands, Cyrul tracked a route through the harsh terrain, and to the sacred spot where Seer had found the first of many Holy Tablets. Cyrul submitted a one hundred fifty-seven-page analysis of Seer's life and travels, making appropriate references to the Holy Tablets and the divine visions that led to their discovery. The Elders had agreed that Cyrul's paper was exceptional.

Cyrul's impressive history put him on the top of the list of Elder Ryman's replacement candidates. Elder Klosik set up a personal meeting late that afternoon, and he welcomed the young man into his office with great enthusiasm.

"I'm honored to be here," Cyrul said as Elder Klosik showed him in.

"Have a seat," Elder Klosik said as he sat down at his desk.

Cyrul sat down, admiring the plush seat. He gave Elder Klosik his full attention.

Cyrul Trevin was a handsome young man with a sturdy, muscular build and piercing blue eyes. He kept his dark, curly hair cut short, as it was favored that way by the Elders. Having chosen the path of the Eldership when it came time to study vocation, Cyrul was accepted by the recommendation of Elder Mosley, whose wife had tutored the boy since adolescence and recognized him to be an exceptionally apt pupil.

"You know why I have set up this meeting?" Elder Klosik asked, although the reason was clear.

Cyrul nodded. "Yes, sir."

"I have a few questions I'd like to ask you."

Cyrul moved to speak, and then decided to remain silent. He didn't want to jump too far ahead of himself and appear too eager.

"You've studied the Holy Tablets extensively," Elder Klosik began. "What did you think of my sermon this morning?"

Cyrul's eyes searched the room for a moment as his mind searched for an appropriate response. He found Elder Klosik's eyes, clearing his throat. "Your sermons are always very inspirational, sir."

"And what do you think of our efforts to restore the Holy Tablets?"

"I believe that you are doing your best, sir," Cyrul answered.

"I've been told that you also were able to memorize the Holy Tablets before they were destroyed," Elder Klosik said, studying the young man's face carefully.

Cyrul looked down. "I'm sorry, sir, but it's clear that I did not adequately memorize the Tablets, as I don't remember them quite exactly as you presented them today."

"I see." A smile perked up from one corner of the Elder's mouth.

"I'll study them harder as soon as they've all been restored," Cyrul added.

"I know you will," Elder Klosik said.

"My only wish is to serve the Eldership," Cyrul said.

"So you accept your nomination?"

"I do, sir."

Elder Klosik gave Cyrul a foreboding grin. "You would be joining the Eldership during a very dangerous time, you know."

"Elder Ryman died because he allowed his faith to falter. My faith is solid. I will help you take down the heathen terrorists." Cyrul now looked Elder Klosik squarely in the eyes, his own gaze unwavering.

Elder Klosik felt sufficiently convinced that Cyrul was his man, but decided to test him with one last inquiry before he made his final decision. "We burn Jode Sadin tomorrow at dawn. I would like you to light the sacrificial pyre."

Cyrul took a nervous breath, but continued to look Elder Klosik sharply in the eyes. "I would be honored, sir."

Elder Klosik installed Cyrul later that evening. The short ceremony began with Cyrul taking vows to the Eldership, and ended with the young man's official name change to Elder Trevin. All Elders went by their formal names, and by shedding one's common name, a new Elder was believed to also shed his or her past as a common person. To become an Elder was to be reborn into a new life—one of wisdom, rule, and privilege.

Chapter VIII
BURDENS OF LIFE

Jeza and Avani kept their voices low as they finished preparing for their walk back to town.

"I think you should just put him to sleep until we get back," Avani said nervously.

"Unfortunately, we can't do that." Jeza felt just as nervous about the venture as Avani did, but she felt she had no choice in the matter. Both agreed that carting him back was out of the question, as they had barely been able to get him to camp between the two of them, the weight too much of a burden to attempt again. But they couldn't simply leave him; if something happened to them while they were away and Jeza was unable to return to him in time, he would surely die out there within a matter of days.

"He could do anything!"

"It's a risk we have to take. I'll knock him out again before I leave him alone with you." Jeza had planned to stay in the Dead Lands for one more day, despite their lack of adequate preparations, but two variables had made that impossible. First, their water supply had gone dry a day early, thanks to Adtom's inability to ration himself. Second, Jeza became aware that an innocent young man was going to be burned at the sacrificial stakes. She fumed at the barbaric interruption and decided she would do whatever it took to ensure the Elders' sacrifice didn't occur.

The two secured their tent and met Adtom in the shade.

"Ready?" Jeza asked.

Adtom nodded. "Lead the way."

The walk was much more treacherous coming back, as they had no water. Thirst overcame them early into their journey across the hot and barren passage. Dusk came, and then evening, but the three continued even as night shrouded the sky with its blinding darkness. Avani and Adtom both stuck close to Jeza, as not to get lost in the black, sandy void surrounding them.

"How much longer do we have to walk?" Adtom demanded.

"We're almost there," Jeza assured them both.

"You've probably been taking us around in circles," Adtom said.

"I know where I'm going," Jeza said with a hint of frustration. "Now, when we get to town, I need you to load up the cart with as many supplies you can. We'll have enough people to pull it easily this time," she said to Avani.

"And what do you want me to do?" Adtom asked.

"I have something I need to do on the other side of town. I'll meet you at the farm when I'm done." Jeza knew she would have to be careful and take her time when she broke into the dungeon, and that she couldn't afford any distractions if she was going to break in and back out of the heavily guarded facility without getting caught. In truth, Jeza bade her time, planning to wait until they got close enough to town before she rendered him unconscious again.

The three continued to walk, and Adtom once again grew restless. "You have no idea where we are, do you? Come on, just admit it!"

"We're almost there."

"Almost there? What exactly does that mean?" he asked, his anxiety visibly transforming into anger toward Jeza.

"Look up ahead and see for yourself!" Jeza beamed, a second wind coming upon her.

Adtom searched, seeing the faintest hint of lights up ahead.

The three sped up, the end finally in sight.

"So, what was the plan?" Adtom asked.

"You and Avani—" Jeza stopped mid-sentence, sensing Adtom's sudden dark thoughts. "No!"

She grabbed Avani and yanked her back in attempt to spare her from Adtom's deadly touch. Adtom reached out and tapped Avani on the chest before Jeza could clear her from his reach.

Avani collapsed onto the sand.

Jeza fell to Avani's side, screaming. She looked up at Adtom. "Why did you do that? She never did anything to you!"

"I've got plans of my own," Adtom said, and then staggered off toward the distant lights. "Don't try to follow me!"

"You had no right! Come back here!" Jeza cried, even though she knew he could not take back what he had just done. "You bastard!" she screamed. "You *bastard*!"

Jeza turned to the dead body that had been Avani and took it into her arms. She began to sob, shaking and heaving with heavy, mournful cries. Of all people, Adtom chose to kill her. Avani . . . gone before she could react. For the first time in her life, Jeza felt alone, vulnerable, and helpless. With all the wisdom in the world, she had not the insight to save the one person who meant the most to her.

Never again would she know another companion as gracious and generous. Never before had the woman left her side. She realized that, as grateful as she was to have had her as a friend, she had also taken her for granted. She remembered her life as a young child, how nurturing and loving Avani had been. Jeza was never her daughter, and yet for many years she relished in playing the role . . . in being loved.

"Please . . . I can't do this by myself!" she wailed, embarrassed at her utterly human response, but unable to restrain herself. "Mommy!" Her heart ached and she sobbed uncontrollably, her body weak and her mind weary. She felt like she, too, might die as she lay holding the lifeless body, crying and cursing, looking up at the distant lights.

She closed her eyes, desperate to remind herself of who she was and why she was there. Her mission was not to be Avani's daughter, but to share God's thoughts with the people, to alleviate them of their ignorance through personal contact and council. Sadly, the people had proved to be far less intellectual than anticipated. For reasons she could not discern, they seemed set on little more than one another's destruction. It made no sense. Nothing made sense. She searched her memories, to a time before she was human, remembering how the people had destroyed themselves time and time again, no matter what God did to try to stop them. Their uncontrollable behavior had been maddening, and yet also so completely intriguing that God would preserve them from extinction every time they had come close to killing one another off.

Jeza had to wonder: If God had created all of humankind out of its own essence, then why didn't every individual feel and recognize the kinship they shared? Why did they continue to fight amongst one another? Even the prophets had somehow completely lost touch with the essence that connected them and everyone else to the original unembodied whole.

Jeza searched her mind for a sense of order in it all as her thoughts shifted back to the lifeless body in her arms, and once again she fell into a fit of helpless cries. Despite whatever divinity that remained in her and the other prophets, they were now just as human, just as fallible and flawed as any other person. Not all of God's combined thought and wisdom could bring back the dead. And yet. . . .

A surge of hope tore through her as she considered the others. She wiped the tears from her face. Still sobbing and shaking, she lifted the body into her arms and began toward town. She stumbled through the sand for what felt like half the night, but finally she made it to the outskirts of town. Her body trembled and ached, but she refused to stop until she reached the Sims' house.

She went to the back of the house and let herself in. She carried the body to the living room, laid it on a sofa, and rushed toward the bedroom. Vara and Ched both slept deeply, lying in one another's arms. Vara woke with a start at the sound of Jeza's footsteps.

"Ched!" she whispered, nudging him.

"What?" he asked, still half asleep.

"Someone's out there!" Vara said.

He sprang up. "Where?"

Jeza rushed in as Ched began toward the door, and he retreated at the sight of her.

Her face was red and swollen from crying. She turned to Vara, her eyes wild and desperate. "Please, you have to help me!"

Ched and Vara huddled together on the bed, terrified.

"You're not welcome here!" Ched yelled. "Leave now!"

"Adtom killed my mother!" Jeza cried. She moved to Vara's side, distraught. "You can bring her back!"

"What are you talking about?" Vara shrieked.

"If Adtom can kill a person, you can bring her back! I *know* you can!"

Jeza tried to pull Vara from her bed, and Ched pushed her away. "I told you to leave!"

Ched began toward the door, but Jeza blocked his path.

"I just want your help," Jeza pleaded.

"If you don't leave now, I'm going to the emergency bell!" Ched warned.

Ched moved back a step as Jeza attempted to

touch him. She lunged, just brushing her fingers across his chest. He fell back, landing on the bed.

Vara began to scream.

"He's not hurt!" Jeza yelled. "Please don't scream!"

Jeza yanked Vara out of bed and dragged her to Ched's sleeping body. "I'll wake him up—after you bring back my mother!"

"What did you do to him?" Vara cried. She shook Ched, trying to wake him, but he continued to sleep.

"I rendered him unconscious," Jeza said. "He's perfectly fine."

"Ched!" Vara cried.

"My mother is in the other room," Jeza said.

"I can't help you! You're crazy!"

Jeza dragged her into the living room, and to Avani's body. Vara buckled at the sight of it. She tried to fight Jeza off, but Jeza threw her to Avani's side.

"Wake her up!" Jeza demanded.

"I can't!"

"You've done it before! I've seen you do it before with your animal friends!"

"They were sleeping!" Vara cried.

"They were dead! You held them in your hands, crying, and they came back to life!"

"No!"

"You know it's true! You *felt* it!" Jeza cried.

"How do you know about that?" Vara finally asked, sobbing.

"Because I saw it . . . in my mind," Jeza said. "I see everything." A deluge of tears fell down her red, puffy cheeks. Her nose ran and she sniffled and coughed like a child. "You can bring her back. Please try!"

Still sobbing, Vara placed her hands on Avani's chest. She closed her eyes, then slowly quieted and became still. She began to feel something. It came naturally. A strange vibrating sensation came to her palms, and then suddenly the pain of Avani's death-damaged body shot through her like a burst of lightning. It pulsated through her veins, nauseating, heavy . . . cold. The pain became unbearable.

Avani gasped as she woke, then cried out as Vara dropped to the ground, coughing and choking. Vara had healed Avani enough to wake her, but she became too overwhelmed by her own body's response to be able to fully heal all of the damage that had occurred while her body had lain dead. Both women now writhed and cried, taken over with pain.

Jeza went to Avani's side. "This is wrong!" she cried. She turned to Vara. "You need to finish healing her!"

"She'll live. Leave me be!" Vara howled as her body slowly curled into a fetal position. She moaned and writhed. "My God . . . God, oh God!"

Jeza turned to Avani. "Everything will be okay." She gave her a hug and willed her to fall unconscious. "Sleep for now." Jeza said, her tears still streaming relentlessly.

She knelt beside Vara, and then offered to help her to a chair.

Vara struggled to catch her breath. "What just happened?"

"It took a heavy toll on your body," Jeza explained, "but you did it. I knew you could!"

Vara rested in the chair, barely able to lift her limbs. She managed to cup her hands over her face and wipe away her tears. "Ched . . . you said you'd wake him."

Jeza nodded, then went into the bedroom and quietly revived Ched.

He jumped up and looked around. "Where's Vara?"

"In here," Vara called weakly from the living room.

He brushed past Jeza, frantically rushing to Vara's side. "Are you alright? What did she do to you?"

"Nothing. Everything's okay," Vara said, still barely able to move.

"She's brainwashed you!"

"Your wife just resurrected the dead," Jeza said, her throat tight.

Ched moved between Jeza and his wife. "Keep your distance!"

Jeza went to Avani's side and gently kissed her forehead. "I have something to do across town." Jeza turned to Vara. "Will you watch over my mother until I return?"

Vara nodded.

"If I'm not back by dawn, go to Len Telan's house. You need to see a very sick woman named Lanora. Promise me!"

Vara nodded again.

"Why us?" Ched asked. "Why do you continue to terrorize my family? People have seen you come here! We've been placed under suspicion because of you!"

"I'm terribly sorry if things have become difficult

for you," Jeza said. "It will all make more sense soon."

"It makes *no* sense!" he fumed.

"Calm down," Vara said, reaching weakly toward him.

"Don't tell me to calm down! We have a heathen terrorist in our house!" Ched yelled.

"I'll be back," Jeza said, moving to the door.

Ched followed her. "You will not!"

Jeza left the house and ran through the empty streets, avoiding guards as she came across them. She kept her focus sharp, directing her attention to the minds of all those directly within her vicinity. By knowing where every nearby guard was, Jeza could ensure her own flawless cover. She crossed the town square and ran through the Worship Hall's main courtyard. The dungeon was close to the Worship Hall, where everyone would be sure to see it. It wasn't a wholly effective deterrent to crime, as the Elders created as many criminals as they prevented, but it was an extravagant display of the Elders' final word.

Jeza sneaked up on the guard at the dungeon gate, rendering him unconscious before he knew she was there. She slid open the shabby, unlocked gate just wide enough to slip her slim body through. She hurried through a dark courtyard. The entry to the dungeon, the only above-ground structure in the large, guarded area, was sealed shut by a large metal door. Three guards marched in formation around the structure, while another two guards stood at the door. All were unaware of Jeza's presence.

She followed her mind's eye, determining her path

by seeing through the eyes of the guards. Strategically positioning herself so she remained out of the guards' direct field of vision, Jeza sneaked toward the dungeon door. There, she charged the two guards and left them sleeping at their posts. She commandeered their keys and quickly entered the dungeon.

The immense underground structure was lit by only a few sporadic lamps hanging from the stone ceiling. Long stretches of darkness filled the cold, wet corridors. A terrible reek of mold hit Jeza as she entered, followed by the nauseating stench of urine and rotting feces. Dull, pained moans echoed from all directions.

Jeza assessed every person as she passed the cells. Although every prisoner begged for freedom, Jeza released only those who were innocent of the charges brought against them. She instructed each person she released to take refuge at her farm.

"There's a hidden room beneath the farmhouse with enough provisions to get you by until I can reach you," she told them. "The door is beneath the rug in the wash room."

Grateful and with nowhere else to go, the escapees complied and followed her detailed instructions.

Jeza reached Jode Sadin, the young man wrongly sentenced to death, in the deepest of the dungeon's cells. She found him praying when she approached the dark cell.

She unlocked the door. "You have to hurry! The next shift of guards just came in, and they found the men I left at the gate. Someone is going to sound the bell!"

"What? What's going on?"

"If you want out, we need to move now!" she yelled.

Wary of Jeza's kindness, Jode stepped out of the cell and followed her toward the entrance. The two moved quickly, but Jeza pushed her tired body to run even faster, as she knew their time was running short.

"No one is covering the eastern gate yet," Jeza said. "Stay close to the wall and we won't be seen."

Suddenly, she tripped over a rocky inconsistency in the hard floor. She cried out as her ankle twisted and buckled on her. A hot, stabbing pain shot through her leg, and her vision blacked out on her for a moment as she tumbled to the ground. *If only stones could think*, she lamented as she turned to the heedless, unexpected mass jutting innocently from the ground behind her. If only stones could think, *she would have known it was there.*

"Help me!" she screamed.

Jode turned back, but he did not stop. Their eyes met for a moment as he offered her a sympathetic glance. "I'm sorry—I don't want to burn!" he cried as he hurried down the corridor.

Jeza tried to get up, but her injuries would not allow her. Not only had she twisted her ankle, but she also had injured her knee on a jagged rock as she hit the ground. Her leg swelled and ached, she felt dizzy, and her senses dulled with the pain. She struggled to remain conscious.

Desperate, she tried to crawl down the passage. Pain seized her leg as she forced it to move her forward. The dizziness increased, and corridor began to spin all around her. She collapsed with a loud cry, writhing and cursing, as two guards ran up to her.

They kept their distance at first, but quickly realized Jeza's vulnerable state. One of the guards quickly moved in, knocking Jeza over the back of the head with the blunt edge of his weapon. "Two months' free tithe!" she heard the man sing as darkness descended over her.

Chapter IX
HEATHENS AND NIHILISTS

Vara and Ched walked down the windy path that led to the Telan house. Both knew of Len's work, but neither had actually seen him or his house, as Len kept mostly to himself and traded very rarely at the town square.

Vara and Ched took in the beautiful sights, admiring the sculptures made of rare gems and fine metals detailing the house.

"They must be very wealthy," Vara said.

Ched looked around, searching for guards. "We should turn around."

"Trust me." Vara stepped up to the front porch and knocked on the door.

Len took his time answering the door. He slowly opened it, peeking out. "May I help you?"

"Jeza Khess sent me. She told me I needed to see Lanora," Vara said.

"Please come in." Len shuffled backward, extending the door completely open. As soon as they cleared the threshold, he shut the door and bolted it with several heavy locks.

"Follow me." Len led Vara and Ched to Lanora's room.

Lanora sat up in bed, trying to eat her breakfast. She stared at the food on her plate, moved it around with a spoon, and watched it get cold. Looking agitated, she set the plate aside, then coughed and spat bloody phlegm into a napkin.

Len entered the room, followed by Vara and Ched.

"Mother, these people were sent by Jeza," Len said.

"I'm sorry, but I'm not really up to talking right now," Lanora said. "Do you know why Jeza sent you here?"

"I think I do," Vara said, going to Lanora's bedside.

"We don't have any clue why we're here," Ched grumbled. "My wife has lost her mind."

Lanora looked up at Vara, confused.

"Just relax," Vara said as she placed her hands on Lanora's chest and closed her eyes.

Lanora grabbed the bed, her body spasming. Her eyes went wide and she gasped loudly.

"What's she doing?" Len asked Ched, alarmed.

"I don't know," Ched answered, frozen in fear.

A light sound escaped Lanora's mouth, not quite a sigh, but more like a whimper, as she watched Vara drop to the floor, gasping and writhing.

"Vara?" Ched called to her as he fell to her side and took her into his arms. "Vara, are you okay?"

Vara cried out, pushing him away. She began to cough and vomit.

Lanora took a deep, painless breath.

"Mother?" Len asked, watching her from across

the room. She had color in her face. Her eyes were no longer sunken in or dulled. She returned Len's glance, then turned to Vara with sudden concern.

Vara slowly got to her knees, and then pulled herself up, catching her breath. She glanced down at the puddle of vomit on the floor. "I'm sorry."

Lanora began to cry. She slid her legs over the side of the bed and eased herself to her feet. Steadying herself, she walked up to Vara and threw her arms around her. "Thank you! Oh dear, sweet child, thank you!"

Ched and Len watched, both of them speechless and still.

Vara moved to the bed and collapsed.

"When did you see Jeza?" Lanora asked.

"She came by last night, late. She said she'd be back, but we haven't seen her yet," Vara explained.

"Was Adtom with her?" Lanora asked.

"No, but my guess is that she went out looking for him," Vara said.

"I would be more inclined to think she had something to do with the cancellation of this morning's execution," Len said.

"Could they have possibly caught her?" Vara asked.

Len shrugged, exchanging another confused glance with Ched.

"Could it be that. . . ." Vara shook her head. "No, she's still alive."

Ched slowly walked up to Vara. "You healed this woman?"

Vara stood, just long enough to fall into Ched's arms. Her eyes welled up as she watched his puzzled face. "If Jeza is a heathen, then so are we. The Elders have misled us."

He held her in his arms, shocked and speechless, then his expression softened and he kissed her on the forehead. "I believe you."

"If Jeza has been taken prisoner, then we need to find some way to get her out," Lanora said. "Do any of you possess any attributes that might help us with that?"

Vara, Ched and Len looked amongst one another.

"I don't have any attributes," Ched said.

"Elder Klosik is your father. There's got to be something you can say to him," Len said to Vara.

"It's not that easy. We're already under suspicion. Trust me when I tell you that the Elders act sparingly when it comes to giving out preferential treatment."

"He had no problem burning his own sister," Lanora said with a slow, troubled nod. "We'll have to think of another way in."

"Are you people insane? We have nothing, no way to save her if she has been apprehended," Ched began. "She's on her own."

Lanora sighed. "I don't claim to know much, but I do know that the five of you came here for a reason. Jeza is the only one of you who even remembers *what that reason is*. If you leave her to die, I fear the rest of you will become even more lost than you already are. Enough people have already died for the truth. You can end this."

Vara, Ched and Len took turns exchanging glances, none really knowing how to respond.

"We sacrificed much to give you the chance we thought you deserved." Lanora turned to Vara.

"Your mother burned at the sacrificial stake for you. Are you going to allow her death to have been in vain?"

Vara looked down. "What do you propose we do?"

Lanora shook her head. "I don't know, but you can't just sit by and do nothing."

"What else *can* we do?" Ched asked.

Lanora smiled. "I have faith that you'll figure it out."

Across town, Adtom hid out in an abandoned shack bordering the Dead Lands. Half of the dwelling was surrounded by sand, while the other half rested on land that bordered the Dead Lands' vast spread. The house had a steep tilt to it, the loose sand having long ago destroyed its half of the heavy foundation.

Adtom gathered together a small stash of food and other goods he had stolen from nearby farms, and opted to eat a ripe piece of fruit. He found a few bottles of bootleg hard cider hidden away on a high shelf in the kitchen. Delighted with the free stash, he opted to partake of the illegal beverage straight from one of the bottles.

He contemplated his current situation and considered simply storming the Worship Hall and killing everyone in his path. The Elders had likely expanded their security, however, and there was no telling how many armed men he would also have to fight off along the way. Adtom understood, much to his dismay, that his body was mortal. As much as he had the advantage over the Elder's guards, one simple mistake could mean his demise just as easily as anyone else's.

Jeza had made a mistake.

Adtom chuckled, recounting his ingenious escape from the woman. The look on her face, the horror and grief . . . how confident she had been only moments before. The impulse had come suddenly, and he had acted upon it so quickly that even Jeza had not the time to respond. By killing Avani, he had sent Jeza a very clear message: *Don't mess with me.*

Avani's death also sent a second message to both him and Jeza: They were fallible. They could make mistakes, despite their superiority, and there were many consequences that none of them were invulnerable to. Despite their varied abilities, they were each also as helpless in their own way.

Adtom was determined to overthrow the Elders and take his rightful place as leader of the people, but he knew that it would take more than sheer will and the touch of death to do that. He needed a plan, carefully laid out, covering every contingency.

He felt the hard cider begin to take effect, and the soothing dizziness normally reserved only for Elders slowly blanketed and dulled his mind. He felt calmer, more relaxed.

He froze as he heard the front door creak open. He swallowed one last bite of fruit, then slowly and silently got to his feet and stumbled toward the hallway. He realized within his first few steps that he was far more intoxicated than he had thought, and he made a painstaking effort to remain quiet as he walked. He made his way to the front of the house, listening to the shifting of floorboards coming from careless footsteps in the entry. He held close to the wall, moving toward the door to the front of the house and waiting beside the door, fighting to silence his heavy, nervous breath.

Jode Sadin sneaked into the room, and Adtom immediately tackled him.

"You have two seconds to tell me what you're doing here!" Adtom snarled.

"I'm sorry! I thought this place was abandoned, I swear!" Jode shrieked, smelling the hard cider on Adtom's breath. "I'll find another place!"

"What are you doing way out here, if not looking for me?" Adtom asked with a paranoid gleam in his eyes.

"Jeza Khess broke me out of the dungeon last night. I was supposed to burn this morning. She said she knew I was innocent."

"Jeza Khess? You know Jeza? Is she a friend of yours?" Adtom asked.

"I never met her before in my life!"

"Do you know where she's staying?" Adtom asked.

"As far as I know, she's now a guest at the Elders' dungeon. She fell and busted her leg. I . . . left her. I didn't want to die." Jode cringed remorsefully.

Adtom smiled. "You did the right thing."

Jode carefully examined Adtom's face, surprised and confused. "I thought you two both led the terrorist group."

Adtom lurched back, letting Jode up. "There is no terrorist group, and Jeza and I are the furthest thing from friends." He returned to the kitchen to finish his fruit.

Jode followed. "Just shows you how much the Elders know."

"I sense a spiritual crisis coming on," Adtom said, pleased. "Have a seat."

Jode sat at the table.

"The Elders were going to burn me, an innocent man, just to give the people a show. 'Spiritual crisis' doesn't come near to describing what I feel," Jode said.

Adtom smiled. "Good. You're waking up."

Jode looked down, just as confused and angry as ever. "Waking up, eh?"

Adtom held out the bottle of hard cider to Jode. "Want some?"

Jode took the bottle, but then set it back down on the table. "Where did you get it?"

Adtom shrugged. "Why should the Elders have all the fun? Come on, live a little!"

Jode reluctantly took a swig of the bittersweet liquid, grimacing at the slight burn it gave to his mouth and throat. "Not bad." He took another large mouthful.

Adtom gave Jode a serious, somber face. "I think we might just be able to help one another."

"How?"

"I say that if the Elders are looking for a war, we give them one." Adtom smiled again, but his eyes remained serious and intent. "So, what do you say?"

"I say you're completely out of your mind." Jode smiled. "You can count me in!"

Chapter X
THE PRICE OF ONE SOUL

Jeza slowly came to. At first her thoughts were too cloudy for her to do much more than comprehend that she was somehow standing up. As the fog lifted slightly, she became aware of the shackles that bound her to the cold, rocky wall, cutting deep into her wrists. She had been hanging there, unconscious.

For how long. . . ?

She winced at a sudden shock of pain in her shoulders, a hot shooting sensation running up her arms and down into her back. She placed her feet firmly on the ground and shifted the support from her arms to her legs. Her injured leg throbbed, proving unable to support her. She shifted her weight onto her good leg, and her knee shook, also threatening to give out on her. She tried leaning against the wall, but it offered her little aid.

Her head throbbed. She couldn't concentrate. She tried to focus on the guards who had found her, so she could see what had happened after she had fallen unconscious. Small bits of their memories came to her, but they felt more like pieces of a fuzzy dream than actual recollections.

She wanted desperately to go back to sleep, but the discomfort emanating throughout her body would not allow her any further rest. She assessed her surroundings. She was in a small room, bars separating her from the corridor leading out. There were no windows, the structure being entirely underground, and there was only one door leading out. Chained securely to the wall, her chances of escape were minimal.

Dizziness took over again and her leg gave out on her. She hung by her arms, limp and shaky. Pain shot through her shoulders and back with even more intensity. The room began to spin again, and Jeza clenched her eyes shut to defer the nausea it threatened to generate. She heard voices coming from the bend in the corridor. She wanted to cry out, but forced herself to remain still.

A guard led Elders Klosik and Trevin to Jeza's cell.

She looked up at the Elders, even though it pained her to do so. She studied their faces and their robes, and realized that Klosik had installed a new Elder.

She also realized that she could not hear either of their thoughts.

She began to panic. She concentrated, but was only able to sense vague images and feelings. She felt helpless. The injury to her head had to have been extensive; the fog that lingered in her mind was obviously affecting more than just her ability to think clearly.

"The infamous Jeza Khess," Elder Klosik began,

his face beaming. "Did you think you could run from us forever?"

"You gloat over a missed step and an injured leg. How humble." Jeza got back to her feet, struggling to hold herself up.

"I'm going to ask you a few questions," Elder Klosik said as the guard returned with a long, leather whip.

The guard handed Elder Klosik the heavy whip, then unlocked the cell door and allowed both of the Elders in.

Elder Klosik snatched the guard's keys. "You can go now."

The guard bowed and marched off.

Elder Klosik handed the whip to Elder Trevin. "Your first lesson in prisoner interrogation, my boy. Give it a few good practice snaps."

Elder Trevin snapped the whip a few times, slowly getting a feel for the long, cumbersome weapon.

"I don't know anything," Jeza said, her voice shaky and timid.

"That's the first thing they always say," Elder Klosik said to Elder Trevin, giving him a nudge.

Elder Trevin cracked the whip, and it sliced into her chest.

Jeza fought to ignore the pain, biting her tongue. She could not let them see her crumble. She stared into Elder Trevin's eyes until he finally looked back, and the two stared one another down.

"I want you to tell us where Adtom Rudin is hiding," Elder Klosik said.

"I don't know."

Elder Trevin cracked the whip a second time.

Distracted by her eyes, his aim fell short and he barely grazed her shirt.

Elder Klosik glared at Elder Trevin, who still met Jeza's defiant gaze. He grabbed the whip from the young Elder. "Don't go easy on her just because she has a pretty face!"

Elder Klosik snapped the whip, slashing Jeza's left cheek. Jeza gave out a horrified shriek.

Elder Klosik handed the whip back to Elder Trevin.

Blood trickled from Jeza's face and down her chin. A few tears found their way out, despite her efforts to hold them back, and they stung as they passed over her torn skin.

"I'm going to ask you again. Where is Adtom Rudin?" Elder Klosik demanded.

"He killed my mother and ran off! I don't know where he went! I swear I'm telling the truth! *Please* don't whip me again!"

Elder Trevin cracked the whip, lacerating Jeza's arm, and she winced as another heavy stream of tears escaped.

Elder Klosik couldn't help but smile. "We'll come back to that one later. Perhaps you can tell me, then, who the other three supposed 'pieces of God' are?"

Jeza scowled at Elder Klosik, holding her mouth tightly shut.

Elder Trevin slashed at Jeza's chest and stomach with the whip, hitting her several times. Her cries echoed throughout the dungeon.

"Three names, Jeza, and he stops."

"Go to hell!" she cried.

Elder Trevin slashed Jeza's legs with three more

cracks of the whip. The pain in her already injured leg suddenly became unbearable, and she couldn't help but go completely limp. The shackles bit into her wrists, causing her to attempt to stand again, but she could not bear the weight.

"I'm going to ask you one more time, and then I'm going to stop being nice," Elder Klosik said.

Jeza remained silent, staring at the floor. Her aching, bleeding body was too heavy to move, and yet somehow she summoned up the strength to get back to her feet. Her body trembled, threatening to give out on her again any moment. She found the young Elder's eyes and stared him down once again.

Elder Klosik waited a moment, his patience growing thin. Elder Trevin looked over at him, unsure what to do.

"Lash her until she stops moving—but don't kill her. We'll get her to break."

Elder Trevin, with only a moment of hesitation, began a relentless onslaught against her, the whip tearing up and down her body, reducing her clothes to bloody shreds.

Jeza collapsed. She tried to put her tortured mind in a place other than where she currently was . . . swimming in the lake on a warm afternoon . . . lounging on the front porch with Avani, drinking cold water and admiring the sweet, cool breeze. . . . The pain became too much to bear, however, and she began to scream hysterically. Her body stiffened and convulsed, fighting the chains and slamming against the hard wall. Then, suddenly, everything once again went black.

She found herself in a dream. She hovered over

her body, and then floated down the corridor, to the dungeon door.

She watched as Elder Klosik ordered the guards to ring the bell in the town square. He had new information he wanted to release to the people. She viewed the Elder from a shallow bird's eye view.

The townspeople slowly congregated, and within a short period of time, the Elder was surrounded by a sizeable group.

"Thanks to your cooperation, we have recently apprehended the heathen terrorist leader, Jeza Khess." Elder Klosik smiled proudly.

The people began to cheer.

"Unfortunately, she refuses to speak," Elder Klosik continued. "We are going to make every effort to get the information we need from her, so that we might take down her entire group. This might take time, but our people are dedicated."

The people roared, satisfied with the short update. Elder Klosik left the crowd, moving down the stone path back toward the dungeon.

Elder Trevin stood over Jeza's swollen, bleeding body. She did not move, but she was still alive. He turned as Elder Klosik returned.

"The interrogation didn't go very well. She passed out," Elder Trevin said. "She didn't even answer one question."

"Every will can be broken."

"I'm afraid I'll beat her to death before she talks." Elder Trevin handed the whip to Elder Klosik, trying to hide the the shame he felt over his violent act. Jeza seemed to have been telling the truth about Adtom, and Elder Trevin had to admire her will to protect her comrades. She was a worthy adversary, if an adversary was what she had to be.

"Don't tell me you're willing to give up so easily."

"No, sir, of course not." Elder Trevin thought quickly. He needed to choose his next words wisely, finding something sharp, something cold. "I'm sure there are other ways we can torture her, ways that aren't immediately life-threatening. We should not have to compromise the quality of pain we inflict just to keep the prisoner alive. We just need to get creative."

"Go on."

"We need to think from her point of view. What do we know about her?"

Elder Klosik shrugged. "She has a farm."

"Burning the farm would be a start."

Jeza suddenly lapsed into a few moments of consciousness, desperately looking up at Elder Trevin. "I can't help you! Please don't destroy our farm!"

"So, she's been listening in on us." Elder Klosik stormed up to Jeza and grabbed her by the face. The wound on her cheek opened back up and began to bleed freely.

Disoriented and confused, Jeza looked up at Elder Klosik. "I heard you in a dream. You said you were going to burn the farm." Jeza felt cold. Her body shook violently. The darkness threatened to engulf her mind once again and she fought to remain conscious. "Even if you do burn it . . . I still won't speak!"

Elder Klosik unraveled the whip and prepared to give Jeza a few more lashes.

Elder Trevin stopped him. "Sir, with all due respect, we need her alive."

Elder Klosik lowered the whip. He gave the young Elder an angry sneer. "Aren't we suddenly the authority on whips?"

"Forgive me, sir. I don't mean to second-guess your years of experience and wisdom." Elder Trevin bowed humbly. "It will not happen again."

Elder Klosik nodded. "Acknowledged."

Jeza began to cry. Her thoughts were a jumbled mess, but she still understood the issue most forefront in her mind: she had failed. The original experiment had taken an unusual turn, and finishing the mission no longer seemed possible. Her only mission now was to survive, or die with her honor still intact. Her human frailties shone through more now than they ever had before, but she refused to let go of who she was: consciousness incarnate, the mind of God. The Elders could do whatever they wanted, but they could not take that away from her.

Elder Klosik watched Jeza for a moment. Even chained to a dungeon wall, her clothes reduced to rags, beaten senseless, she still had an air of dignity to her. It made the Elder's blood rage. He glanced over at Elder Trevin. "You have a nice new house, six bedrooms, a fully stocked kitchen," he began.

"And I thank you and the Eldership for such a generous gift." Elder Trevin bowed.

"How would you like a concubine to keep you company in that big, lonely new house of yours?" Elder Klosik asked, raising his brows and looking back over at Jeza with a wicked grin.

"I'm no one's whore!" Jeza screamed, fighting the

chains, clinging to consciousness by only a thread.

"Sir, the Holy Tablets clearly state that 'all whores shall be judged by their Elders.'"

Elder Klosik chuckled. "That's true, my boy. And those words hold very significant meaning. I personally have five whores in my house, and I happily judge at least one of them every night."

Elder Trevin laughed along with the older man for a moment, but then fell somber once more. "But sir, how dangerous do you think it will be for me to keep her?"

Elder Klosik thought for a moment. Finally: "You are an Elder now. Don't tell me that you don't feel God's wisdom and special grace flowing through you."

"I do feel it, sir," Elder Trevin lied.

"She's yours now. Do with her as you like—drug her, torture her—as long as you get the information we need. This is my first test for you as an Elder. I'm confident that you will not fail me."

Elder Trevin bowed. "I would be honored to take Jeza Khess into my house as my concubine. I will not fail. I will break her, sir."

"I will not break!" Jeza cried, fighting the spinning room once again. "And you . . ." Jeza searched her tangled mind for the correct string of words. "You can still go to hell!" She thought to spit on Elder Klosik's shoes, but she was too dehydrated to produce the sputum.

Elder Klosik laughed and Elder Trevin followed suit. Elder Klosik took the young man by the shoulder. "You have your work cut out for you."

"I will enjoy putting her in her place, sir."

"I'm sure you will."

Jeza angrily yanked at the chains, then collaped with a pained cry.

"How will I transport her, sir?"

"I say you chain her up and move her now, while she's weak," Elder Klosik said.

Jeza hung limp, wishing she had the strength, any strength at all, left within her with which to fight. "Please, just kill me," she cried, not even bothering to look up. "I am of no use to you, not anymore. And you clearly have nothing to offer me. There's no reason for me to continue living."

"I'm sure Elder Trevin will find at least one good use for you before you die, my dear." Elder Klosik gave Jeza one last crack of his whip, and then left to get the guards. "Make sure she doesn't go anywhere," he chuckled.

Jeza's body felt like it was on fire. She couldn't tell how many times the Elders had lashed her, having gone nearly senseless after the sixth or seventh crack of the whip.

Was this worth a man's life? she wondered. A man who wouldn't even stop to save her, after all she had risked? She shouldn't have come for him. She should have weighed his virtues more harshly. She should have been able to foresee Jode's ultimate worth.

And then there was Adtom . . . her timing wouldn't have been so rushed if he hadn't sidetracked her with Avani's brief death. Because of him, Jeza stood to lose everything she had lived for.

She screamed in a fit of rage. Despite the mind-numbing pain and impending shock, she began to fight the chains. She swung her arms, yanking and pulling, screaming and howling. Her senses dulled and darkness blanketed itself around her, but she continued to fight. Finally, trembling with fatigue, she had no choice but to give in to the calm, dark void. She fell limp, hanging by the chains tightly clasped around her bruised and swollen wrists, her battered body showing only the faintest evidence of the life that now only barely clung to it.

The Elders watched as the guards lowered Jeza from the wall and bound her in a new set of chains, then carried her out of the dungeon.

Jeza woke on a plush bed, wearing nothing but a robe. There was a chain secured to her good leg, which in turn was attached to a large metal ball that lay on the floor. She looked around, straining to correct her blurred and distorted vision. Scrawling trails followed along her line of sight, as if her eyes were somehow sketching out hazy lines on a transparent canvas before her. Her vision moved in slow reverberating increments, a confusing distortion of the smooth movements with which her eyes usually moved. It made it difficult to stand, balance, and even direct her limbs with any degree of coordination.

A single lamp lit the room, which was decorated with fine draperies and statuettes. It suddenly hit her that she was in the home of an Elder.

The newly acquired home of Elder Trevin. . . .

She tried to focus, her weary head threatening to black out on her yet again. She got to her feet, taking a moment to steady herself, and she began to limp toward the door. She looked down at her swollen leg. The pain was minimal, which surprised her, considering the bruising and extensive swelling. She got as far as the metal ball would allow her, and then attempted to drag it. The sudden pain that shot through her bad leg was enough to make her knees buckle, and she crumbled to the floor.

She gathered the robe tightly around her and curled up where she was on the cold wooden floor.

She closed her eyes. Her mind shifted to the irony of her sudden captivity. She had traded in her life, and for whom? Jeza shook her head. What was the possibility that Jode would try to return for her? Was there even the slightest, even the most remote chance, that he saw enough value to her innocent life, just enough, to risk his in an attempt to save hers? She cursed the limitations of her broad awareness, wishing she had the insight to see the future of her decisions.

The anger returned, and her thoughts suddenly returned to Adtom and all he had done. She felt such disgust by the thought of him that she had to shun the image of his face from her mind's eye. She wondered where each of the men could be when her mind suddenly fell into a dulled, confused state. Her head began to throb, and then everything began to go numb. "Damn the both of you," she muttered, fighting tears again.

Chapter XI
THE FALLEN

Adtom and Jode hid behind a large patch of brush near a clearing, waiting a short walk away from the abandoned shack, watching a nearby clearing. Dina and Vetho Onlan, a young married couple, quietly approached. Dina was a petite woman with modest looks and long hair. Vetho was short, stocky, and not at all attractive, and he walked with a slight limp. Both lugged large bags on their backs, the few personal belongings they would be carrying into their new life.

"It's them," Jode said, exiting the brush.

Adtom held back, allowing Jode to approach them first and ensure that they were alone. There was certainly a price on Adtom's head by now, and he was cautious about the possibility of an ambush.

Dina and Vetho both jumped, startled, as Jode emerged from the bushes. Dina put her hand to her heart. "Jode! You just about gave me a heart attack!"

"I'm sorry. Adtom doesn't trust anyone these days." Jode turned to Vetho, and the two shook hands.

"Glad to see you again!" Vetho said. "You truly must have the luck of the devil!"

Jode smiled. "I told him all about you two. He's very eager to meet you."

"Well, show the way," Vetho said.

Jode led the couple off the path, and the three met Adtom behind the brush.

"We're clear," Jode said with a smile.

Adtom extended his hand toward Vetho, and the young man cringed back. Adtom chuckled at the reaction. "I take it you saw my little performance in the town square."

Vetho and Dina both nodded.

"Fear is good. It's healthy. However . . ." Adtom extended his hand out a bit further. "So is owning a good pair of balls. You're going to shake your new leader's hand, I hope?"

Vetho nervously extended his hand, and he and Adtom shook.

"That wasn't so hard, now was it?" Adtom extended his hand to Dina, who courageously offered hers without hesitation. Adtom took her hand, but kissed it instead of giving it a good shake. "It seems that your wife might be holding your pair in her purse."

The men laughed, Vetho sheepishly following along.

Dina blushed. "If I carry my husband's balls, sir, it's only to keep their precious cargo safe."

Adtom and Jode burst out in a huge fit of laughter.

"I assure you he is an honorable and brave man," she continued.

"I'll have to take your word for it," Adtom replied,

still taken by Dina's quick wit.

"I told you you'd like them," Jode said eagerly.

"Let's get back to the house. This calls for a feast," Adtom said. He led the way, with Jode proudly walking right behind him. Vetho and Dina followed, apprehensive yet excited.

The Onlans had lost almost everything they owned to the Elders. They had fallen behind on their tithe and were subsequently ordered a ten percent penalty on top of what they already owed. By the time the next collection came, Vetho and Dina had fallen into what the Elders called criminal debt. They had no choice but to relinquish their land to the Elders, suddenly living in their own house under a lease they had been forced to sign. Everything they earned on the farm now belonged to the Elders. Vetho and Dina had been blessed with magnificently fertile land, and yet they found themselves left with barely enough food to survive.

The Elders were not holy people, Vetho and Dina both knew. They had lost their faith long ago, and yet they had continued to go to Worship Hall sermons and town meetings—because attendance was required. They paid their tithes, kept quiet, and tried to remind themselves that things could always be worse.

Up until a couple of generations ago, the world had been in a nearly constant state of war, but the believers of the One True God crushed the heathens. Before that, the believers had warred with and destroyed the nihilist empire in the battle that had prompted God to create the Dead Lands. The Elders declared themselves victors of the Holy Wars, and the people took it as a sign from God when the Dead Lands suddenly stopped spreading.

A mere coincidence, Vetho and Dina both knew. The Elders needed to be stopped, and if anyone could stop them, it would be Adtom. They followed their new leader to the small shack, abandoning their allegiance to the Elders as they entered the tattered building, blind to the even greater lie that now led them into the dark room and into the dark reaches of their minds. They were young, rebellious, and impressionable—just the types of souls he could infect easily with his angry, senseless cause.

"So, will we be destroying the dungeon first?" Dina asked, looking eager to get her hands dirty.

"I thought we would start with Elder Klosik's estate," Adtom said.

"But what about Jeza Khess? The Elders have her," Dina said.

"Let her burn," Adtom said.

"But why?" Dina asked.

"Why not?" he asked, his eyes challenging her.

"How long does it take to plan an attack?" Vetho asked.

"Plan?" Adtom chuckled. "We just storm the place, kill anything that moves, and blast everything in our path."

"But there will be guards . . . with weapons," Vetho said.

"Are you questioning my abilities?" Adtom asked.

"No, I just thought—"

"Don't think, just do," Adtom interrupted.

"Can we take back our farm?" Dina asked, barely able to contain her excitement. She began to laugh uncontrollably, the hard cider getting the better of her.

"We'll force them to give up more than just your modest farm, my dear," Adtom said, smiling at her with a wink.

Vetho frowned.

Adtom got to his feet, feeling that his new followers would likely expect some sort of initiation ritual to solidify their allegiance. He thought for a moment, hoping something simple yet effective might come to him. He began to improvise. "Tonight, I declare you my brothers and sister. I release you from the laws of the Elders and offer you a future of leisure and wealth. Swear your allegiance to me, and I will lead you to victory."

Jode was the first to stand, followed immediately by Dina and then a very apprehensive Vetho.

"Once you swear your lives to me, there's no turning back. I want to make sure I'm clear."

The three initiates nodded.

"Jode," Adtom began, "do you denounce the Elders and offer your allegiance, your life and your soul to me?"

"Yes," Jode replied.

Adtom turned to Dina. "Dina, do you denounce the Elders and offer your allegiance, your life and your soul to me?"

"Yes." Dina smiled.

Adtom glared over at Vetho, raising his brow. "Vetho, do you denounce the Elders and offer your allegiance, your life and your soul to me?"

"Yes," Vetho said, his voice quavering.

Adtom smiled. "We are now brothers and sister." Adtom motioned for them to sit, and the three took their seats.

"No, not you." Adtom gently pulled Dina from her chair. "You get to come with me."

"Where are you taking her?" Vetho asked, clearly no longer enjoying himself.

"To the bedroom, of course." Adtom put his arm around Dina and began to walk her away from the table. Dina did not resist him, but she still moved nervously and with hesitation. She turned back to Vetho, her eyes begging him to say something.

"That's my wife!" he said, jumping to his feet.

Adtom turned back. "The vows you two made to one another in front of the Elders mean nothing here. You vowed your lives and your souls to me, didn't you?"

Vetho nodded, helpless.

"Prove your allegiance to me, and you will never know poverty again. Cross me, and you will pay with your life and your soul," Adtom said.

Vetho held his breath, watching horrified as Adtom caressed Dina's body, staring him down.

Vetho turned away. "You could have any woman. Why my wife?"

Adtom began to fondle Dina though her clothes. "Because she is no longer yours to claim."

Dina closed her eyes, her face going flush.

"Let's go," Adtom said, and then led her into the bedroom.

The door shut behind them.

Chapter XII
BONDS OF THE FLESH

Vara rushed frantically to get dinner ready for the stove, second-guessing her rash decision to have the Klosiks over.

Ched pulled a stack of plates from a tall cupboard, and set them down on the counter. "This is a really bad idea."

Vara rolled her eyes. "We can't cancel on them now!"

"What if they decide to take a look at the workshop? I think we should move her—"

"She's fine where she is," Vara interjected. "They've never taken an interest in your work before. What makes you think either of them would want to go back there tonight?"

"For all we know, they're planning on searching this whole place while they're here."

"My mother—" Vara paused for a moment. She took a deep breath. "She's a good woman. She wouldn't let anything like that happen."

"Not even she can stop the Elders once they've set their suspicions on someone. Vara, we can't go through with this! They'll know something's up as soon as they look at you!" Ched began to pace.

The scenario was ludicrous. They had Jeza Khess' comatose mother lying on the cot in his workshop, the head Elder was due to arrive for dinner at any time, and Vara was about to face the man whom she now knew was responsible for her mother's death.

Ched turned to her pleadingly. "Vara, you're a wreck."

"Worry about yourself. I'll be fine!" Vara chopped vegetables, lining the bottom of a baking pan.

"I just don't see any benefit to having them over. He's not going to say anything, and the risk we would be taking by even mentioning Jeza's name is huge."

"We're not canceling!" Vara continued to chop vegetables as she glared up at Ched. She cursed aloud as the knife slipped, slicing one of her fingers. She pulled back her hand, quickly healing it, and then sat down for a short break.

Ched went to her, putting a hand on her shoulder. "Calm down."

"Calm *yourself* down!"

Ched knelt down, so that he and Vara were at eye level. He took her hands into his. "We're both on edge, and we have good reason to be. Let's not take it out on one another. I'll do this with you . . . but you need to compose yourself."

Vara nodded. The two embraced.

"I'll give the house one more run-through, just to be absolutely sure we're presentable." Ched kissed Vara on the lips and left the kitchen.

Vara got back to her feet and continued cooking.

When Vara heard a knock at the front door she stayed in the kitchen, leaving Ched the burden of letting in the Klosiks. She began to shake, as if the Elder might arrest her for her very thoughts. She arranged a plate of appetizers and steadied her breath as she heard Ched open the front door. With another deep breath, she carried the plate into the living room.

Elder Klosik and Lauru sat on the sofa as Vara approached them with a nervous smile.

She offered them the appetizers. "I'm so glad you were able to make it!"

The Klosiks sampled her appetizers—simple, flat cakes, not the sweet fruits and expensive pastries they were accustomed to. Vara watched for their approval.

Lauru smiled. "These are very good. You'll have to give me the recipe."

Satisfied, Vara set down the tray and took a cake for herself.

"At least we know you eat," Elder Klosik said.

Ched bit his tongue.

"We really don't do this often enough," Lauru said.

"No, we don't," Vara agreed.

There was a moment of uncomfortable silence. Vara and Lauru both opted for another appetizer.

"Dinner should be ready soon," Vara said.

"Good—I'm starving," Lauru said with a smile.

More silence. Lauru tried to pretend she was interested in the humble décor. Elder Klosik turned away from his hosts to yawn. Vara grabbed Ched's hand, desperate for his comforting touch.

"So." Elder Klosik turned to Ched. "How has business been?"

"It's been a little slow, but we'll come up with our next tithe somehow." Ched smiled. "I need to start building less reliable clocks, or I might go out of business." He laughed, and Vara laughed with him.

"We could use a new clock," Elder Klosik said. "Couldn't we, love? Maybe we can glance through the shop before we leave tonight?"

Lauru coughed, annoyed. "That's a fine idea."

Vara and Ched both paused, each waiting for the other to answer.

"I couldn't possibly expect you to buy one of my average, everyday clocks, sir," Ched began, thinking quickly. "If you need a new clock, allow me to build you something custom to match your home."

"What a fantastic idea!" Lauru sang with a clap of her hands. She gleefully finished her cake.

Vara stood, releasing Ched's hand. "I'm going to go check on dinner." Vara hurried out.

"I'll help." Lauru followed Vara into the kitchen.

Vara peeked into the wood-burning stove, already knowing that dinner was not nearly as close to ready as she had suggested. Elder Klosik's presence suddenly terrified her, and she had to retreat from him for a moment. He was not her father, but rather the lying imposter who had murdered her birth mother. He was currently attempting to have information tortured out of Jeza, no doubt. Who knew what low he would stoop to next?

"You seem like you have a lot on your mind," Lauru said, looking genuinely concerned.

"I guess I'm still not over Father suggesting that I was seen talking to terrorists. What's gotten into him lately?"

"He's just on edge with everything that's been going on. Please try not to take it personally."

"Wouldn't you?"

Lauru conceded with a deep sigh. She quickly turned to the stove and peeked inside. "Looks good."

"Thanks." Vara began to dry and stack dishes. "So, I guess Father has Jeza Khess in prison? That's good news, right?"

"He celebrated all night with the concubines."

Vara looked down. "Do you know when they plan on burning her?"

"You know your father never discusses those kinds of things with me."

Vara shrugged. "I was just curious. She's all the town is talking about right now."

"Thank God they caught her when they did, that's all I can say."

Vara nodded.

Ched yelled from the living room. "How dare you go back to that again? It's because of *our* tip that you identified their leader!"

"Don't you raise your voice at me, boy!" Elder Klosik roared.

Vara and Lauru hurried back into the living room.

"What's going on?" Lauru demanded.

"He was fishing for information about the heathen terrorist leader!" Elder Klosik yelled.

"That's not true!" Ched shouted even louder.

Lauru moved to the Elder's side. "I'm sure you two just had some kind of misunderstanding."

"He was fishing!"

"Father!" Vara tried to remain calm.

"I have a duty to the people above all else, even

my family," Elder Klosik said. "I've collected intelligence on this house, things that I can now confirm!"

"Stop now!" Lauru yelled. "If you don't, I will never forgive you!"

Vara and Ched exchanged glances. All eyes slowly fell on Elder Klosik.

"Do I have to count my own wife among my enemies now, too?" the Elder asked.

"No, love," Lauru said, taking him into her arms. "You're tired. You've been working too hard. You need a good night's rest . . . to clear your head."

Elder Klosik hugged her back. "Perhaps you're right." He glared at Vara and Ched over Lauru's shoulder.

"No more talk of politics," Lauru said. "Tonight, let's talk of family, of home, and of a bright and happy future."

Everyone nodded, although no one looked at all at ease, and once more the room filled with a disconcerting silence.

Chapter XIII
ENEMY MINE

Jeza looked around, disoriented and groggy, her vision still blurred and distorted. It took her a moment to realize that she lay on a wooden floor and Elder Trevin stood directly over her, watching her.

"Sleep well?" he asked.

Jeza quickly sat up, clasping her robe shut with both hands. She felt dizzy, her mind even more clouded and jumbled than before. She felt as if her life had somehow slipped into an overwhelming, surreal nightmare.

"I took the liberty of bathing you and dressing your wounds while you were still unconscious."

"My head. . . ." Her words trailed off as she struggled to think.

"It shouldn't hurt."

"Something's wrong," she said, terror seizing her as she realized that the awful silence still filled her mind, the accustomed din of others' thoughts, dreams, and memories seemingly lost to her.

Elder Trevin lifted Jeza into his arms and gently

laid her onto the bed. "Do you remember your name?" he asked.

"Huh?" she asked, her heart racing as she attempted to tap into the Elder's consciousness.

"Your name," he said. "Do you remember who you are?"

She felt his hand on her stomach as she lay on his bed, her ankle chained and her mind alone, and she found herself fighting fearful, angry tears. "My name . . . is Jeza Khess," she said. She struggled again to focus her mind, and a wave of dizziness fell over her.

"You're not going to try to incapacitate me?" he asked, sweat beading up across his nervous face.

The reminder sent Jeza on the offensive, and she struggled to focus her thoughts just long enough to render the Elder unconscious. Her mind began to spin as a violent seizure sent waves of chaotic misfires through her every limb.

Elder Trevin watched, stepping back and allowing her to seize uncontrolled. After only a few seconds, her convulsions slowed and her body relaxed. She stared ahead for a moment, barely conscious, barely able to move. A thin trickle of drool ran down her chin, but she chose to ignore it, too exhausted mentally to perform the physical feat of wiping it away. She watched as Elder Trevin stared her down with a satisfied smile.

"I've taken the liberty of having you lobotomized—not severely, mind you, but enough to keep you in your place," he said, looking proud of himself.

Jeza closed her eyes. "Let me go."

Elder Trevin chuckled as he threw open Jeza's

robe. He touched her breast, and then tried to kiss her. He began to shake, hit with a sudden sense of excitement and nervousness, his expression one of both arousal and terror.

Jeza turned away. She struggled to focus her eyes, and the dizziness began to spin her jumbled mind even faster.

"You belong to me now." He moved to her ear, lowering his voice to a whisper. "If you please me, maybe I will find a way to spare your life."

He removed his formal robe, exposing and fondling himself.

"No," Jeza said as he climbed on top of her.

She closed her eyes, concentrating again with all of her will on rendering the man unconscious. Her mind grew even weaker, her confusion and dizziness escalating out of control. Her body seized once more, her mind falling into a stinging incoherence. Her sanity threatened to slip away, leaving her in a strangely silent void. She screamed, angry and terrified as she went still, her mind broken. Somewhere in the distant reaches of her thoughts, she heard Elder Trevin laughing.

She felt the warmth of his body against hers, and it came to her that she was helpless to stop him from advancing upon her. Driving her legs open with his own, Elder Trevin forced himself inside her, thrusting hard and deep, tearing through the virgin tissue with a pleasured groan. She cried out, unable to fight him off. With no strength to stop him, she lay helpless as he drove himself further into her. She tried to take her mind elsewhere, but every thrust brought her back to him and the carnal offense he imposed against her.

Then, suddenly, he froze, shaking and moaning. He lay against her for a moment, holding her close, and then he left her alone on the bed, immediately donning his robe.

Jeza lay, crying and shaking, a mixture of blood and semen trickling out of her and onto the bedsheets.

"I do hope that you have a change of heart and start cooperating with the Eldership," Elder Trevin said, caressing her still exposed body. "It would be a shame to see this pretty body burn."

She closed her eyes, turning away from him.

"You should be grateful that I took pity on you. You could still be in the dungeon, subject to Elder Klosik's whip."

Jeza's mind was a mess of frustrated, confused thoughts. "The Eldership . . ." she began, and then forgot what she wanted to say. "You . . ." she tried again, and then couldn't find the words.

"The Eldership is good to the people," Elder Trevin said.

The thought returned for a split moment as she looked at the blood still flowing from her, and the irony of her new enslavement made Jeza burst into a frenzy of laughter and shrieking cries. At once, she fell silent, too tired to continue. She gazed forward, her jaw slightly agape.

"Maybe we can convert you," Elder Trevin continued. He got up and then began toward the door.

Jeza's mind worked to comprehend what the young Elder had said to her. She turned to face him, slowly grasping his words. She took a moment, searching her mind for a rebuttal. "But I'm God," she finally said, unable to come up with a more sophisticated response.

"You're my whore," he corrected her.

"No. . . ." She realized that her body was still exposed, and pulled her blood-soaked robe around her.

He stopped and turned back at her as he reached the door. "Do you know how to cook?"

"Huh?" Jeza thought at first that he had to be talking to someone else.

"My mother always made all of my meals. I need someone to cook for me."

Jeza moaned, rolling over. She felt a strange sense of disassociation, like her body was no longer her own. Even her thoughts felt distant, just beyond her reach. When she did grasp them, they seemed jumbled, nearly nonsensical. Beyond the confusion, it seemed as though nothing else existed. Nothing made sense.

Elder Trevin watched as she stared ahead, dazed and unresponsive. She began to drool again. "Jeza?"

His words echoed through her, and then were gone as quickly as they had come.

The Elder tried to make eye contact, but she looked past him, searching for something that was no longer there.

"Did you hear me?" he asked.

She looked up at him with a start, her head spinning. "Huh?"

"I said, *did you hear me*?" he yelled, shaking her.

She closed her eyes and covered her ears. "I hear *nothing*—nothing at all!" She tried again to pry into Elder Trevin's thoughts, and immediately fell into another violent seizure.

The Elder backed out of the room. He watched from the threshold until Jeza's body went limp, then he shut and locked the door.

Chapter XIV
BUSINESS AS USUAL

It was the first day of the new month, and the Elders sat in their business chamber seeing people, case by case, who had grievances to be settled or information they wanted to share. Today had begun particularly tediously, and the Elders all seemed to be in especially foul moods.

The chamber had tall vaulted ceilings. The windows all stood well above the head of even the tallest of men, sending in outside light in, but without allowing a visitor to peer in or out. Dark shadows filled the far corners, making it feel cold and ominous, and the tall stone-encrusted door was heavy and solid. It felt as if the chamber might have been an annex to the dungeon itself, although the two structures were not immediately connected.

The Elders spent the morning seeing those who had made appointments, and then contributed the first part of the afternoon to last minute drop-ins. The Elders sat, all of them on edge, as a guard showed in the next case. An older man stood with his son, a young man just reaching adulthood. It was clear that they both wore their finest clothes, which were still rags compared to the fine robes and silk sashes worn by the Elders.

"State your case," Elder Klosik said.

"Sir, I have a dispute with my neighbor and I am afraid it may affect my ability to pay my tithe," the older man said, trying to hide his shaking hands. He clasped them behind his back, acting as if he might appear more formal that way.

"What is your dispute?" Elder Forese asked.

"My neighbor refuses to fix his fence, and his livestock are coming into my fields to graze. My crops are suffering, ma'am," the old man replied, his eyes shifting about the room.

"And why won't he fix his fence?" Elder Forese asked.

"He says he doesn't have the materials or the money for it."

"Then why don't you build a fence of your own?" Elder Forese asked.

The older man looked down. "Because I don't have the money, ma'am."

Elders Klosik and Forese exchanged glances.

"Ma'am, I brought my son as my witness." The older man moved his son forward and in front of him, as if the boy might function as some sort of protective shield from the Elders' icy stares.

"It's true," the boy said.

"I only wish to rectify this problem so that I may pay my tithe on time," the older man said.

Elder Forese nodded. "And you shall have no problem. I will sign a statement for you to deliver to your neighbor. Until he fixes his fence, you are free to do with the livestock on your property as you see fit. They are yours to slaughter, to sell, or to shear for yarn."

The older man moved his son aside and bowed to the Elders. "Thank you, ma'am!"

Elder Forese wrote a short note under her official letterhead and signed it.

The guard retrieved the note and handed it to the older man.

"We expect your tithe on time now, with no excuses," Elder Klosik said in a commanding voice. "We have given you a generous exception. If you should fall delinquent any time from this day forward, you will forfeit your son to the Eldership."

The older man gasped, pulling his son close to his side. "I will not fall delinquent, sir."

Elder Klosik signed a note under his letterhead, and handed it to the guard. "Please have this filed."

The guard nodded, then showed the man and his son out.

"Did you see the looks on their faces?" Elder Klosik asked Elder Trevin with a chuckle.

Elder Trevin mimicked a look of shock, and then laughed along.

The guard brought in a young woman next. She had a painfully shy face, and stared at the ground as she stood before the Elders.

"State your case," Elder Klosik said.

The young woman attempted to look up, but still failed to reach Elder Klosik's eyes. "Sir, I have reason to believe that Kano Labur is conspiring with the heathen terrorists."

"And how do you know Mr. Labur?" Elder Sanell

asked.

The young woman was hesitant. "He's my betrothed."

Elder Sanell nodded. "What is your evidence?"

"Well . . ." The young woman cleared her throat. "He came to my window the other night. He was supposed to be in the dungeon. He said that Jeza Khess had broken him out."

Elder Sanell sat up in her seat. "Did he tell you where the terrorists were staying?"

"Yes, ma'am."

Elder Sanell waited for the young woman to continue, and then impatiently prompted her to continue: "Are you going to tell us?"

The young woman took a deep breath. "They're staying at the Khess' farm."

"No, we've already searched the place. It's been deserted."

"They're there . . . unless he lied to me," the young girl said.

"So you've come to me with unconfirmed evidence?" Elder Sanell grumbled.

"I can definitely confirm that Kano knows Jeza Khess, although I cannot prove it, ma'am."

"We'll make a note of it. As for presenting hearsay about the farm, I'm going to leave it up to Elder Klosik as to whether or not we will hold you in contempt."

The young woman finally looked up, her eyes pleading. "Sir, I only mean to help you in the Eldership's cause against the heathen terrorists. Please consider my information about the Khess farm as a lead, and not—"

"Miss . . .?" Elder Klosik asked, interrupting her.

"Colia. Miru Colia, sir."

"Miru, I will consider your information a lead, and nothing more. Elder Sanell will send her people to the farm once again. If she finds no one there, you will be held in contempt." Elders Klosik and Sanell both immediately jotted notes under their specific letterheads, signed them, and handed them to the guard.

The guard placed Miru in a restraint.

Miru became hysterical. "I have a child at home! You can't arrest me! I came to help you!"

"You'll be released if your information is correct. If not, we will schedule your sentencing at a later time," Elder Klosik said.

"Sentencing? But sir, I've done nothing!"

"That will be all," Elder Klosik said.

The guard took Miru by the arm and marched her to the holding room.

Elder Klosik turned to Elder Sanell. "After they search the Khess farm, tell them to burn it."

Elder Sanell nodded, and then scribbled away at another order.

The guard returned. "That was your last case, sir."

"Thank you." Elder Klosik sat back in his plush chair with a relieved sigh. "You can close the door behind you."

The guard bowed and closed himself out of the room.

Elder Klosik turned to Elder Trevin. "Any news from your lovely guest?"

"Nothing yet. She has begun to speak a little."

"And what about her sleeping spell?" Elder Klosik

asked.

"The lobotomy has impaired her thoroughly," Elder Trevin answered. "She is no more a god or demon now than she is a babbling idiot."

The other Elders laughed.

"She can try to disable me—and trust me, I've already given her more than one reason and opportunity to try," Elder Trevin continued, his voice going bold.

The Elders nodded, impressed.

"She will soon find that she has no recourse, and also that it is ultimately in her best interest to cooperate. We will find her conspirators, with or without her help, but if she does aid us, I beseech the Elders that they might be persuaded into offering her leniency," Elder Trevin said.

"You know that we can't really offer her that," Elder Klosik said.

"Right, of course not, sir," Elder Trevin said, the disappointment evident in his voice.

"Is she coherent enough to question?" Elder Sanell asked.

Elder Treven shrugged. "It might be too early to tell."

The Elders nodded amongst themselves, satisfied. A lobotomy, when performed by a skilled surgeon, could disable a person to varying degrees—or render the subject completely incapable of any reasonable or intelligent thought. The Elders had made it clear that they wanted Jeza left with some communication ability, but also that they needed her brain damaged enough to render her incapable of performing her mental tricks.

"I want to question her about Ched and Vara Sims," Elder Sanell said. "I have several witnesses who claim to have seen Jeza Khess at the Sims' house on more than one occasion. I would like to know more about both of them before I attempt to make an arrest."

Elder Trevin nodded.

"Do we have any other business to discuss?" Elder Klosik asked.

Elder Sanell cleared her throat. "I would like approval to increase the guard. With times like these, we need to consider the possibility of a terrorist revolt."

Elder Klosik nodded. "Approved. Any other news?"

"I have the finance report finished. We have seven households that have not yet paid last month's tithe, sir," Elder Forese said.

"Have you sent out summons?"

"Yes, sir."

The Elders all turned as the guard knocked on the door.

"We're still meeting!" Elder Klosik yelled.

"I have a messenger, sir. He says it's urgent," the guard called from behind the closed door.

Elder Klosik threw down his paperwork and sat back with a frustrated sigh. "Send him in!"

The messenger hurried in.

"This had better be important!" Elder Klosik growled.

The messenger handed his note to the guard, and then nervously watched Elder Klosik read it.

Elder Klosik's face slowly grew red, and then he

slammed his fist into the desk. "You can go!"

The messenger and guard both hurried out, and the door slammed shut behind them.

Elder Klosik looked over at Elder Sanell, his face suddenly going from bright red to ashen. "The heathen terrorists have burned down my house. My wife is missing. The servants are all dead. My guards caught one of them . . . one of the terrorists. He's waiting for us in the dungeon."

Vetho Onlan stood in a dank, smelly cell, bound to the wall by thick chains. A small rodent had targeted Vetho's bare feet as its next meal, and Vetho kicked the relentless creature across the cell. It shook its head, recovering from the blow, and then began to slowly inch its way back toward his bleeding toes.

The rodent ran and hid as Elders Klosik, Sanell, and Trevin followed a guard up to the cell. Elder Klosik carried a whip in one hand and a lit torch in the other.

The guard unlocked the door.

Elder Klosik handed the torch to Elder Trevin and entered the cell. He snapped the whip, lacerating one of Vetho's ears. "Where's my wife?"

Vetho cried out. "I don't know!" Vetho began to bellow and moan, his severed ear bleeding heavily.

Elder Klosik lashed Vetho repeatedly, lost in a blind rage. "You're lying!"

"No, please!" The river of blood began to deafen Vetho's severed ear.

Elder Klosik continued to snap the whip across Vetho's hot, red body.

"Please!" Vetho screamed. "She . . . wasn't

there!"

Elder Klosik let the whip fall. "Why did you burn down my house?"

Vetho sobbed and moaned, unable to catch his breath long enough to answer.

"Do not make me repeat myself!" Elder Klosik yelled, his voice thundering through the cell and corridors.

"Adtom," Vetho cried.

"What about Adtom?" Elder Klosik snapped the whip, skillfully missing Vetho's eye by scarcely more than a hair's width.

Vetho jumped, clenching shut his eyes with a startled scream. He looked down, horrified, as he lost control of his faculties and soiled himself.

"Talk!" Elder Klosik yelled.

"He made us do it!" Vetho began to wail hysterically.

"And why did you go along with him?" the Elder demanded.

Vetho began to shake. His voice began to quaver. "I don't know!"

Elder Klosik handed Elder Trevin the whip and traded it for the torch.

Elder Klosik walked up to Vetho. "Do you know Vara and Ched Sims?" he asked, holding the flame dangerously close to the man's face.

"If you say so!" Vetho cried.

"Is that a yes?" Elder Klosik asked, moving the flame even closer.

Vetho screamed as his skin began to singe. "Whatever! I don't know! For God's sake, stop!"

Elder Klosik pulled the flame away, but still held it

uncomfortably close. "Tell me how you know Ched Sims!"

Vetho struggled to come up with something quick, his mind reeling. He cried aloud. His face was wet with blood and tears. "I . . . don't know!" he cried. He stared at the torch, shaking and sweating. "I'll say whatever you want! Please—just stop!"

"Back to question number one: where's my wife?" Elder Klosik asked.

"I don't know!" Vetho cried.

Elder Sanell entered the cell. "Where are you hiding out?"

Vetho began to hyperventilate. "A shack . . . south border . . . on the edge of the Dead Lands!"

"Do you know Jeza Khess?" Elder Trevin asked.

Vetho shook his head. "No!"

"Do you know of her affiliation with Adtom Rudin?" Elder Sanell asked.

Vetho hung his head, weakened from the burning, sharp pain emanating from his ear. He couldn't respond. He couldn't stop sobbing.

"Yes or no?" Elder Sanell raised her voice.

Vetho nodded.

"Do they belong to the same terrorist group?"

Vetho shook his head.

The Elders looked among one another.

"That's consistent with Jeza's story," Elder Trevin said. "Looks like we could be dealing with two groups."

"You wouldn't be lying to us for any reason, now, would you? Maybe to mislead us?" Elder Klosik asked Vetho, threatening him with again the flame.

Vetho shook his head violently, crying out. "No, I

promise!"

Elder Sanell turned to Elder Trevin. "When do you estimate that we will be able speak with Jeza?"

"Soon."

Elder Sanell nodded. "I'm going get my people started on our new leads. Elder Trevin, could you please set up advertisement for guard recruits?"

"Yes, ma'am."

"I'll arrange a trial for tomorrow," Elder Klosik said, glaring at Vetho. "I'll have a messenger deliver you all of the details by this evening."

Vetho watched the Elders leave, and then stared at the guard as he locked the door.

"Hey!" Vetho yelled as the guard began down the corridor.

The guard stopped. "What?"

"Help me, please!"

The guard shook his head and continued on his way.

"Have some pity!" Vetho cried, barely able to breathe. "I don't want to die!"

"You're the one who is going to burn, not me," the guard said with a shrug, then disappeared down the corridor.

"I'll pay you!" Vetho screamed. "Please!"

Vetho waited, but the guard did not return.

He considered the fact that he was likely going to burn at the stake unless one of Adtom's people proved noble enough to rescue him. Dina might make an attempt, he knew, but there was a good chance that not even she would risk her life to save him. He hoped that burning to death would not be as horrific as it looked, that his body would quickly go numb and his mind would go swiftly.

Vetho had not believed in God for a long time, but a deep fear in the pit of his stomach forced him to pray anyway. He desperately needed someone, anyone, to hear his plea. He had no idea that his prayers were, indeed, going to someone very specific. He prayed, unaware that his heartfelt words simply became an added piece of garble in the jumbled, captive mind of his leader's alleged enemy. Vetho prayed in the dark, putrid dungeon cell, his words echoing through the rocky corridors and then waning into the oblivion of Jeza's dark cerebral void.

Chapter XV
REPRISAL INFERNO

L en stood among a few other young men and women before Elder Sanell. He had received word that the Elders were looking for new recruits for their guard, and now he stood to join. He knew that Jeza was most likely in the dungeon, and a guard for the Elders would have the closest access to most of their restricted areas. He had only met Jeza once. He really didn't know her, but he did know that Jeza had convinced Vara that she could heal, and sent her to restore Lanora to health. For that alone, Len was in Jeza's debt.

Lanora had urged Len on. Jeza's mother, Avani, who had been Lanora's friend for many years, still lay in the deep slumber in which Jeza had left her to finish healing. Vara had finished the task, then she and Ched had moved her under cloak of darkness to the Telan home for her own safety. Now, Jeza was the Elders' prisoner and everyone who knew anything was under suspicion.

Len stood in a daze, listening to Elder Sanell as she called out the names of her new recruits. Each potential guard replied in turn, answering random questions as she posed them. She had a paranoid look to her, one like Len had never before seen, and he struggled to suppress his shaking limbs and hold his composure as she finally reached his name.

"Len Telan," she called out, her finger holding her place along the stiff parchment as she read her list.

Len stepped forward, and he took a deep breath as all eyes suddenly fell upon him.

"Why do you want to join the guard?"

"My life has been unfulfilling," he replied.

"Alchemy is a worthwhile profession; at least it has been for you," Elder Sanell said.

"There are things in this world more important than gems and precious metals," Len said, and then immediately he wondered if he had crossed the line. He held his breath as he waited for the Elder to respond.

"Tell me, in your own words, what that might be," she said.

"The truth," he answered, fearful.

Elder Sanell thought for a moment, and then nodded, satisfied with his answer. He breathed a sigh of relief as she moved on to the next name on her list. "Heith Messa?"

A brawny young man raised his hand, looking just as nervous as Len. "Yes, ma'am."

"Why do you want to join the guard?"

He looked around for a moment, as if his neighboring recruits might offer him the answer. He cleared his throat as he shifted his eyes to address the Elder. "Ma'am, I've wanted to be a guard since I was a little boy, ma'am. Now that the terrorist heathens threaten our right to worship the One True God in peace, the time just felt right, ma'am."

Len listened intently as Elder Sanell made her way down the list, each recruit offering a similar reason for joining and each one being accepted without further question. She dismissed the small group, and they marched to a training area on the town's east border. The facility was geared toward turning youths of all types into dedicated soldiers, and was also a prerequisite for applicants hoping to become future Elders. The course consisted of combat training and religious studies combined with mind-altering tactics such as sleep deprivation and hypnosis.

Signing up for the guard meant vowing lifelong servitude to the Elders. Those who could not pass the training courses were sentenced to become servants and concubines. Those who attempted to escape their fate were beaten, lobotomized, or killed.

Len had thought he had known what he was getting himself into; however, he had no idea how grueling the process actually was going to be. Orientation was an eye-opening event. Len stood among the group as the lead training guard began to speak about the Guard and its head officer.

Elder Sanell, one of only a handful of women to ever make it into the Guard, had dazzled her superiors at the time with her gift for tactics, logistics, and strategy. She had quickly climbed the ranks, finding herself in the position of lead guard for her predecessor, Elder Nemes, within a year of her first assignment. Elder Nemes personally groomed Sanell for the position, aware of his own terminal illness, determined to fill his seat personally.

Elder Sanell took over the Guard with seamless grace and quickly proved herself as a God-chosen leader. Like Elder Forese, Elder Sanell was not allowed to marry. A female Elder could not be expected to function throughout a pregnancy, nor with a child at her teat, and she was therefore forced to sacrifice marriage and children for her position. She was a model for Eldership dedication and loyalty, the guard explained to the new recruits. She was, he told them, what every guard strove to be.

Len stood silent. He stared at the speaking guard, pretending to hang on the man's every word.

At the Khess Ranch, the guards helped themselves to fruits and vegetables from the untended fields as they watched the house burn. They cheered as the roof collapsed into the house.

Inside the house, everything that Jeza and Avani owned burned. No memory was spared. The interior of the humble structure was a striking contrast of black smoke and bright, blinding fire. Anything that could burn was ablaze.

Under the house, the prisoners Jeza had rescued huddled together in a secret cellar. As debris from the fire fell overhead, it obstructed the trap door, their only exit. Smoke poured in through the floorboards, and the refugees choked and gasped for air. They tried to push open the door, but it was no use. They were buried alive. Panic filled the dark, smoke-filled room. Arms reached out in desperate flails, only to claw blindly at neighboring flesh. Oily soot covered skin and filled lungs. Bodies crumbled over one another, wretching and twitching. Then the building collapsed, stifling their screams.

Across town, bordering the Dead Lands, guards searched Adtom's abandoned shack. They were unable to find anyone on the property, although they did find two recently emptied bottles of hard cider. The guards cleared the property and began to leave. On a tall nearby hill, Adtom, Jode, and Dina watched the guard leave.

"I knew he'd talk!" Dina said, her voice distraught.

"Then good riddance!" Adtom said. He smiled. He would enjoy watching Vetho burn.

There had been a few public burnings since Adtom had been an adult, but he had never personally witnessed one. His father had strictly forbade him to go, threatening to banish him from the house if he defied him. He had called Adtom morbid for wanting to see such a spectacle.

Now Vetho would burn, however, and no one would be there to stop Adtom from attending.

With the shack searched and the Khess ranch reduced to cinders, the guards headed north, filing through the pathway leading to the town proper. As they reached the first few inhabited houses, no one noticed Lauru diving into the lush bushes in front of the Sims' house.

Lauru watched the guards pass, mindful of the extra guards placed on the area, and dashed into the back yard. She searched for any potential prying eyes as she made her way to the back door. She tried it, grateful to find it unlocked. She hurried through the door and quickly closed it behind her.

Vara jumped to her feet as Lauru ran up to her.

"I was on my way to the Worship Hall for—"

"Mother, what's wrong?" Vara asked, helping Lauru to a chair.

"—when I heard them talking about you!" Lauru continued. "You have to get out of here! There are guards all over this place!" Lauru handed Vara a piece of folded paper. "This is their route. Don't let them see you!"

"I don't understand!"

"They think you and Ched are heathen terrorists!"

"I thought we had already settled that!" Vara cried.

"It doesn't matter! You need to pack your things and disappear now!"

Vara's heart sped up, and a deep panic began to come upon her. "Where do we go?"

"I don't know." Lauru gave Vara a kiss on the cheek. "I'm sorry, but I have to go. They'll notice I'm missing!" Lauru rushed out, struggling to keep herself composed.

"Wait!" Vara began to go after her, but stopped herself as she thought better of it. She turned and hurried instead to Ched's workshop.

They decided to head for the Telan house, unsure where else to go. As they prepared to leave, they could hear the distant ring of the town square bell.

It was time for Vetho Onlan to burn.

Chapter XVI
HIEROPHANTS AND FOOLS

Lauru and Elder Klosik stood over the ruins of their home, both still overwhelmed by the sudden loss. They had lived there together for over thirty years. Now their home, their life, had to be rebuilt from scratch. The Eldership would provide for them, and for that they were thankful.

"I've issued an order for Vara's and Ched's arrests," Elder Klosik said, his words collected and calculated, as if he had not been thinking about the house at all.

"I think you're making a mistake." She turned away from the demolished mansion. "I think everyone is."

"What the hell is that supposed to mean?"

Lauru gazed into her husband's eyes, her own sad and sincere. "You know the Elders never burned any pregnant virgins at the sacrificial stakes. The five women who burned together died for your political agenda, not for the Eldership! Keep your stories straight for the people, love. I am not the people; I am your wife."

144

He turned away, defeated. He shook his head, hesitant to reply.

She put an arm on his shoulder, trying to look understanding. "Please talk to me," she said.

"We should have looked harder for them, Lauru! Vara should've burned in Nalia's womb!"

"Vara is a good person! And so is Ched! You've allowed the heathen stories to turn you into a paranoid, hateful tyrant! The hysteria of the terrorist attacks has everyone pointing their fingers in all sorts of ridiculous directions! You are supposed to be the voice of reason! Instead, you fuel the madness!"

He slapped her across the face, and her eyes dared him to try slapping her again.

Surprised by the response, he stood down. "You are my wife—you're supposed to support my endeavors!"

"Vara is my daughter, and—"

"Vara crawled out of the womb of a dirty whore!" he interrupted.

"Listen to what you're saying! Have you no sense of love for anyone other than yourself?"

"My love is for the Eldership," he said.

"And what about me?" she cried.

"And what *about* you?" he cried back. "You ask for nothing, your every need taken care of by the Eldership! What more do you want from me?"

"I want you, my love," she said, her voice growing faint, her energy spent.

She embraced him, desperate for his affection. He hugged her and kissed her, but quickly and evasively, and then he pushed her aside, smoothing his robe. "I have to go. I have an appointment with Elder

Trevin."

He sent for his cart, leaving Lauru with two guards for protection. The two would make sure that Lauru got to her temporary home safely, (and without making any unwanted stops). She knew Elder Klosik had become paranoid even of her. He trusted no one completely, not even his fellow Elders. He felt a looming sense of impending doom. Someone was going to try to overthrow the Elders, and very soon. He could feel it, and his feelings shone through in every decision he now made.

Elder Trevin eagerly welcomed Klosik to his new home, and showed him to his lavish living room. Red silk draped across the windows and to the floor, and plush sofas sat around a heavy, wooden table. Each sat on opposing sofas, and they watched one another for a moment across the table.

"Would you like something to drink? Juice? Hard cider?" Elder Trevin asked.

"Water would be fine," Elder Klosik said with a smile.

"Jeza!" Elder Trevin called toward a distant room. "Bring in a glass of water!"

About a minute or so passed, and then Jeza slowly made her way into the room, carrying a glass of water. She wore a modest dress, had her hair down, and went barefoot. She had her ankle wrapped up, and she painstakingly dragged the heavy metal ball behind her.

"It's for Elder Klosik," Elder Trevin told her.

Jeza handed the glass to Elder Klosik. She recognized him, but just barely.

"Have a seat," Elder Klosik told her.

She sat down beside Elder Trevin.

"I see you can understand me." Elder Klosik glared across the table at her.

She nodded, then turned to the wall and began to stare intently.

"I want to ask you about Ched and Vara Sims," Elder Klosik said.

Jeza did not respond to him. She continued to stare at the wall, her eyes fixed on something that seemingly only she could see.

"Jeza?" Elder Trevin asked. When she continued to stare, he placed a hand on her shoulder.

Jeza jumped, as if snapping out of a trance. "Huh?"

"Elder Klosik wants to know what you can tell him about your friends, Ched and Vara."

Jeza thought for a moment, her eyes shifting over to look at each of the Elders. "I don't know them."

"What do you know about them, then?" Elder Trevin asked.

"I'm not sure," she said, closing her eyes. For one moment, she remembered who she was. For that one moment, she saw all, heard all, felt all, remembered all. . . . For that moment, she saw the universe for what it was, the people for who they were, and her life for what it was, and everything made perfect sense . . . for just that moment.

And then it was gone.

Tears filled her eyes. "I don't know anything!"

"I think you do," Elder Klosik said, his eyes piercing and angry.

She shook her head, feeling confused and tired.

She realized that the entire left side of her chin was wet with drool, and she wiped it away as her tears wet her cheeks in its place. She let the tears go, unashamed of those. Her tears at least *meant* something.

"You went over to their house," Elder Trevin tried, gently redirecting her eyes to his. "Remember?"

She tried to glance back over at Elder Klosik, his look too horrifying and unpredictable to ignore, but Trevin held her fast.

"Tell me what you remember," he said, his free hand going to her lap.

She watched his eyes as she struggled to think. "I went over to their house," she began.

"And then?" he asked.

"Adtom killed my mother!" she shrieked, suddenly in a panic. She shook her head, quickly calming. "No . . . she's not dead. Vara brought her back."

"Vara brought her back from the dead?" Elder Klosik asked, astonished. A glimmer of excitement hit his eyes.

Jeza turned to Elder Klosik, nearly processing the damage she had just done, and then she turned back to Elder Trevin. "May I go lie down now?" she asked him. "I'm very tired."

Elder Trevin turned to Elder Klosik and, after receiving the affirmatory nod, he allowed her to take her leave.

She found her way to the soft bed and collapsed, her body still spent from all the Elders had collectively done to it. Her wounds from Elder Klosik's torture still stung and swelled, and seemingly despite them, Elder Trevin had ravished every other untouched inch that was left of her. He took her all night sometimes, his appetite for her unsatiable, and he was like a terrible fire that tore through her, slowly burning away at both her body and her soul.

She fell unconscious and her mind drifted to a place she had known before, back when she was whole. Then, she realized that she was watching, perhaps dreaming, Adtom and Dina running together through the forest.

The two ran and giggled, running around trees and jumping over small bushes and patches of flowers. Adtom carried a bottle of hard cider, and the both of them were very drunk.

"No one saw us!" Dina laughed. "You are a genious."

Adtom and Dina found a comfortable, secluded spot and fell back onto a thick blanket of clover.

"At least they didn't reward him for snitching on us," Dina said.

Adtom nodded.

She suddenly began to cry. "I can't believe he's gone!"

Adtom took Dina into his arms. "Don't cry. You know it's all for the best."

"Is it? Really?"

He kissed her softly yet passionately. "You know it is. Now, lie back and relax. I think we could both stand for some physical release."

"You're *always* looking for some physical release!" She turned away, tired and shaken.

"Come on, now," he said, his voice changing, almost echoing. "Roll on over."

Elder Klosik?

Jeza felt a hot, scorching pain on her right outer thigh, and she cried out as the pain snapped her back to her dulled senses. *Elder Klosik was branding her.* Skin came off like melted cheese as he lifted the hot brand and pulled it away. A painful, round welt began to rise where the skin had been seared.

"I'm sorry, my dear, but he insisted," Elder Trevin said, standing nearby. "All living property has to be marked."

She turned away as hot tears rushed out.

"I think she's had enough for one day," Elder Trevin said, moving to her side.

"Don't start going easy on her just because you've let her into your home," Elder Klosik said. "She's your slave—"

"And you gave her to me to interrogate as I saw fit," Elder Trevin interrupted. "Have I not provided you with enough valuable information?" he asked. "I would think you would have a few more important people to interrogate right now—such as your 'daughter' and 'son-in-law.' Please don't let me keep you," Elder Trevin said, glancing suggestively at Elder Klosik.

Elder Klosik nodded, suddenly looking strangely thoughtful. "Let me know if you get anything else out of her."

Elder Trevin nodded back with a smile. "I'll be sure to do that."

Chapter XVII
TO PROTECT AND SERVE

Len stood in formation, his legs shaking. He had been on his feet all day, performing drills and jogging, and he didn't know how much more his body would be able to take. The guard instructing his group noticed Len's difficulty and pulled the young man out of formation. "What's a scrawny, tiny guy like you doing joining the Guard, eh?"

"I'm hoping to build some muscles, sir!" Len said.

The other recruits laughed, and the guard's face grew red.

The guard swept Len's legs, throwing Len off balance and to the ground. "Perhaps you'd be better suited for dance lessons instead."

The recruits' scorn flipped immediately to Len, the laughs intermingled with comments degrading his masculinity. A couple of commentators in the back of the room began to take bets as to whether Len would begin to cry.

To everyone's surprise, Len got back to his feet. He looked the guard in the eyes, swallowed hard, and took a deep breath. Everyone there seemed to hold their breath with him as he contemplated his response, and then the group released a collective sigh of relief as Len asked, "Could you teach me that move, sir?"

Everyone watched, silent and curious.

The guard took a moment to respond, then nodded and repeated the move slowly until the moment of impact so that everyone could see more effectively the mechanics. Len returned to the ground. He took a moment to force the wind back into his lungs, and then climbed to his feet.

"Thank you, sir," Len said, still working to catch his breath.

The guard nodded. "Lesson over. You're all wanted next in hall five."

Staying in formation, Len's group began to march toward hall five. It would take them only a few minutes to get there, but Len's legs burned with such fatigue that he felt like he might not make it.

Stay on your feet! Len yelled silently to himself. Left, right, left, right . . . each step one step closer to the hall. His legs grew heavier with every step and his feet dragged, but he continued to march in time with his group. *Almost there*, he told himself as the building came into sight. He wondered if any of the other guards in training were suffering as badly. If they were, they hid it well.

The group approached the hall and filed through the open door. Len entered, relieved to find desks had been set up for lecture. He chose the closest chair he could find and collapsed into the seat. He stretched his legs and back, his body stiff and achy.

He felt as though he might melt into the hard, wooden chair and fall asleep.

A guard walked in and shut the door behind him. "The topic we will be reviewing today is heathen mythology and its continued threat to the Eldership and the people." He moved to the head of the room and faced the class. "Any questions before we begin?"

No one dared move.

"The heathens, more specifically the followers of the so-called 'Holy Books' written to blaspheme the Holy Tablets, were once thought to have been expunged by the Dead Lands. Now, of course, we know this is not the case. The original five Elders, champions over heathens and nihilists alike, taught us that only believers of the One True God deserved to live—and when they did, the Dead Lands miraculously ceased to expand. As long as the Eldership continues, God will bless us and the Dead Lands will remain stable. As guards, it is our job to protect those things that are most precious: the Elders and the truth they offer the people. Just like theirs, our service is to God before all else!"

The young men began to cheer, a thunderous din of excitement filling the room. Len played along, although he took the guard's words very differently than had everyone else. Unlike the rest, Len had not been raised to put his faith in the Elders. Starting from a very young age, Lanora had taught Len to think for himself and never to take anything anyone said, even an Elder, for granted. Far too many people did just that, he noticed, a fact that became increasingly apparent the wiser and more mature he became.

The guard continued his speech, and Len pretended to be taken in by every word. He kept his head straight, no matter what the guards threw his way, masters of propaganda as they were. He wouldn't allow himself to forget why he was there, why he had joined.

He was going to find Jeza Khess.

A messenger entered the room and approached the guard. He handed the guard a note, and then left with a humble bow.

The guard took a moment to read it. He looked up, his eyes wide with anger and surprise. "I've just received word from Elder Sanell, herself. Her intelligence has uncovered that a heathen spy sits among us, right now!" The guard looked around the room. "How many of you have a trained enough eye to spot him?"

The youths began to look among one another.

Len knew that the guard had to be talking about him. He looked around to see if anyone else could tell, hoping no one noticed his sudden, profuse sweating and hot, flushed face. He did his best to retain a calm appearance, but a sickening panic had his limbs shaking and his body ready to collapse. He realized that he was coming close to hyperventilating and forced himself to take slow, deep breaths.

"How many of you paid attention in class? Think about the criteria!" the guard said. "What might he look like? What kind of person would the heathens send to infiltrate such an elite group as ours?"

Len looked around, certain that he would faint any moment, until he realized that many of the other prospective guards also perspired and trembled. It seemed that Len was not the only one there who feared persecution, wrongful or otherwise.

"No one here has what it takes, then!" the guard yelled. He began to scream into random faces. "You all might as well quit right now and resign yourselves to lives of slavery!" The guard eyed the few female trainees in the room. "You'll make fine whores for the new Elder! Go! Leave now! You don't have the spine to be a guard!"

One young woman began to cry. She ran to the door and guards immediately apprehended her as she tried to flee.

"Who else is going? Who else is ready to give up and become a slave?" the guard in front yelled.

Everyone looked around, eyeing the rest of the room, waiting for someone else to make a move. Suddenly, a young man stood and pointed at someone sitting very close to Len. "That's him! That's the spy!"

The others watched hesitantly, looking unsure.

"Well?" the guard in command yelled. "Are you just going to sit there?"

Len fought the urge to vomit. His hands clenched into tight fists, and then suddenly the ground began to shake. He looked around, just as surprised as everyone else.

"Get him!" another yelled. Len braced himself for the attack as the group swarmed in on the accused. He tried to hide his astonishment as the others began to beat the man sitting just to his left.

The young man was muscular and had a very large build, but he could not fight off the group. He looked around, surprised, as they secured his arms behind his back. "Me? You're wrong!" He turned to his peers. "It's not true!" he cried.

"Why are you holding back?" the guard yelled. "Show him how we treat traitors around here!"

"No!" the young man yelled, but no one listened. The group stormed him, several hands holding him secure while the massive mob swung and kicked. Len joined them, as to not look suspicious, his heart aching. He wished he could save the poor man, but there was nothing he could do. The accused fought back with everything he had, but to no avail. With their bare hands, the group beat him until all that remained of him was a lifeless, bloody mass. All went silent, the earthquake falling still.

"Get him out of here!" the guard yelled. "Take him off somewhere out of the way, where his body might rot or be consumed by the beasts!"

The group took the body outside and marched it toward the border of the forest and the Dead Lands. They discarded the body as if it were trash, dropping it under a low-hanging tree, then turned back toward the training camp.

The rest of the day was a confused blur, the event too traumatic for Len to shake. He followed along as the guards moved his group through various other drills, lessons, and exercises, and then he collapsed into his cot when he was finished for the day. He fell asleep almost immediately, but his was a restless sleep riddled with nightmares.

He dreamt that the Elders had sent others in his training group to kill him. He ran, but he couldn't shake his pursuers. They wanted him dead, just like they had wanted the young man in hall five dead. Somehow they had found out that Len did not belong after all, and they intended to do to him what they had done to their previous target. As the mob closed in on him, he felt his body grow slow and heavy, as if he was trying to run while wading through water. The group ran with unimpeded speed, however, and it only took a moment for them to take him to the ground.

He kicked and struggled, but he could not protect himself from the numerous blows coming from all directions. He cried out, but in vain. He continued to struggle, but to no avail. His death felt imminent.

He startled awake, crying out, as a loud bell marked the beginning of a new day. As he became aware of his surroundings, he realized that again the ground was shaking. He sprang to his feet to a din of screams and chaos as the group took cover beneath the beds. Len scurried beneath his bed, praying that the quake would subside before it caused any damage or injury.

All went silent.

The youths stared from under their beds and blankets as a guard entered their sleeping quarters.

"Anyone care to explain what just happened here?" the guard asked.

They looked amongst one another, silent and confused, waiting for someone else to answer. *It hadn't been a quake?*

"No one saw anything?" the guard asked.

No one responded.

"It *looked* like something exploded in here," the guard said. "I saw the whole thing from outside."

The youths all shook their heads.

The guard rolled his eyes with a sigh. "No one heard the bell, either, I suppose?" he asked.

The trainees emerged from beneath their beds, one by one, Len included. Still, no one offered the guard an explanation.

"Get dressed, all of you! Breakfast starts in five minutes. The food is first come, first served, so if you want to eat, I suggest you move quickly!"

Len rushed to get dressed. He felt as though he might pass out and die if he didn't get any food today. His stomach felt as if it might possibly cave in on itself if he missed just one more essential meal. He threw on his boots, tying them quickly, and then made a dash for the food hall.

The guards served a thin gruel to the eager trainees. Len got in line for a serving.

The line quickly grew, and a couple of larger men from a different group tried to pull Len from the line and take his place.

Len reclaimed his spot. "What's your problem?"

"For a little man, he sure has some attitude!" one of the larger men said. He tried to push Len back out of line, but Len shifted is body to avoid the blow and quickly swept the man's legs. He went to the ground.

Len stood, waiting to see if anyone else would make him defend his spot.

The larger man got to his feet. "Nice move." He offered Len his hand. "I'm Dese."

"Len."

The two shook.

The line began to move. Shallow bowls began to fill as they passed under the steaming ladle. There wasn't much of a scent to the food, but it would serve its purpose. Len and Dese came up to the front of the line, eagerly holding up their bowls. They were among the last few to be served, and they ate quickly. The gruel had almost no flavor and had a lumpy consistency that repeatedly triggered Len's gag reflex, but he forced it down anyway. He took the bowl to his mouth, drinking the last of his meal, and still his stomach ached for more.

He longed for home. Lanora was at home, no doubt worrying about him, and he was off studying religion and playing war games. For a moment, he questioned his decision, but his resolve returned as he thought about Jeza.

The guards worked endlessly to break the young trainees. One or two cracked each day. The guards became increasingly ruthless as time went on, pushing Len and the others to their physical limits. They deprived Len's group of sleep for days at a time, then starved each of them a meal for every hour they slept when finally offered a bed. The group was forced to endure endless hours of propaganda speeches. They ran through drills and obstacle courses until they collapsed. With each passing day, the breaking point became nearer for each of them; some slowly went insane, others collapsed so far within their broken psyches that only a shell of their former selves remained. Len's group soon dwindled to half its original size.

Len, however, was determined to get through the guards' trials with as much of his mind left as intact as possible. He knew that quitting wasn't an option, but if he didn't improve his endurance, he would be surely forced into doing so. What he lacked in endurance and strength, he needed to make up in perseverance. There would be an end to it all, he reminded himself. This, like all things, was only finite.

Chapter XVIII
THE EXCEPTIONAL CARRY ON

The Elders sat in their chamber, conducting their weekly personal business. Elder Klosik was tired and distracted, making his mood especially foul. He had people working on his house at all hours, determined to show his enemies exactly how little they could affect him. In truth, he was obsessed with capturing the threat and watching every last element of it burn. He couldn't sleep, he could barely eat, and he could think of nothing but the satisfaction he would derive in having his final laugh.

"Do you have any further leads?" Elder Klosik asked Elder Sanell.

"None, sir. I'm afraid the leads have all gone cold."

"And what about the Sims?"

"Someone had to have tipped them off, but none of our people saw anything. According to our surveillance, no one has entered or left the Sims' house for days."

"How can that be?" Elder Klosik asked.

Elder Sanell shook her head. "The house was

under constant surveillance. I don't know how they could have gotten past our guards."

"Unless they had someone's help," Elder Klosik said, peering across the room with a suspicious eye.

"Who would help them?" Elder Sanell asked, clearly offended.

"Who has the guards' rotation list?" Elder Klosik asked.

Silence.

"Maybe you helped them," Elder Mosley said, turning the suspicion to Elder Klosik.

Elder Klosik leaned back, his hand going over his chest in shock and dismay. "Me? You cannot be serious!"

"Who would you suggest?" Elder Mosley asked.

The two stared one another down, the tension in the room growing with each passing moment. Everyone waited to see what Elder Klosik would say or do next, no one daring to mention the violent twitch that now possessed the Elder's right eyebrow.

Finally, Elder Sanell broke the silence: "We're all getting sidetracked, and I think it's setting all of us off of the real mark."

"And what's the real mark?" Elder Klosik asked, his lips tight and his eyes wild.

"When the terrorists burned your house, neither you nor Lauru were home, correct?"

"Get to the point," Elder Klosik said.

"Perhaps the terrorists meant to send a message rather than kill you," Elder Sanell said.

"What kind of message would be more important than killing the enemy?" Elder Forese asked.

Elder Sanell thought for a moment. "They want to

show us how unafraid they are of the Eldership. They don't think we'll call their bluff."

"That's possible," Elder Mosley said.

Elder Klosik nodded.

Suddenly there was a loud rumble. The Elders looked around, unsure of what they were hearing.

The walls of the Worship Hall began to crack, then parts of it began to crumble. The Elders got up to run as the ceiling began to cave in on them. Windows shattered. Walls exploded.

The Elders ran through the Worship Hall, dodging pillars and rafters. The entire Worship Hall seemed to be collapsing into itself. Dust and debris clouded the air. The Elders made it to safety, just in time to watch the entire building finish crumbling into a disturbing sculpture of rocks and dust.

Adtom stood among the ruins. "I have a tablet for you to add to your collection." Adtom motioned to Jode and Dina, who carted in an enormous stone tablet. The tablet towered over them, and the weight of it was burdensome even for the two of them carting it together. The inscribing had been done masterfully. Jode and Dina leaned the blasphemous monstrosity up against the side of the Worship Hall ruins and ran off.

It read, "Death to all those who continue to follow the teachings of the Elders."

Adtom scrambled up the Worship Hall ruins and stood atop the rubble, looking down upon the Elders. "Stand down and bow to your rightful leader!"

The Elders did not move.

Guards began to file around the Worship Hall, and Adtom retreated with a daring leap and a mad dash for the forest. A handful of guards followed him, but none followed close enough to apprehend him. He slipped from their sights, and they reluctantly returned to the ruined Worship Hall to report the bad news.

There was a haunting silence as the Elders assessed the damage. The guards all tried to look as protective as possible, but none could wipe the terror from their faces.

"Go back out there and find them!" Elder Klosik yelled.

The guards looked amongst one another, each waiting for another to move first.

"Cowards!" Elder Trevin yelled as he charged alone into the forest.

Two guards pursued and the rest quickly followed suit.

Four Elders stood by the ruins. Elders Klosik toppled the offensive tablet with an angry thrust, and it cracked into several pieces as it hit the ground. He turned to Elder Sanell. "Increase security at all of our remaining properties. How many new guards do you have at the training facility?"

"I could have ten or fifteen to you by the end of the week," Elder Sanell said.

"Any chance for more than that?"

"Not if you want them all properly trained."

"Find a way," Elder Klosik said. "Your men are resourceful."

"With all due respect, sir, we can't start making rash decisions just because—"

"We are at war!" Elder Klosik interrupted, slamming his palm into his fist. He drew closer to

Elder Sanell, so that his face held less than a foot from hers. "We *will* see to it that every one of our enemies dies screaming and begging for mercy. And I will be there, to stare into their eyes and damn their souls as their bodies burn and reduce to lumps of rotting coal!"

Elder Sanell swallowed hard, and then turned away. "I'll gather as many guards as I can. I'll be at the training camp if anyone needs me." She stormed off.

Elder Klosik turned to the remaining Elders. "Dismissed."

The two Elders looked at one another, neither seemingly knowing where they should go. Elder Sanell stood where she was, still shaken from Adtom's attack, while Elder Mosley began to tug and topple the rubble, seemingly intent on clearing the site with his bare hands.

"Go home!" Elder Klosik yelled, visibly shaking. He looked around, shocked to find a small group of onlookers. "*Everyone* go home!"

Elder Trevin ran through the maze of trees and brush, searching for Adtom and his followers. He froze as he heard a horrified shriek coming from somewhere in the near distance.

Slowing his pace as he heard yet another cry, this time closer, he looked around, watching, listening. He jumped as another nearby guard emitted a painful wail.

"Sir!" A guard ran up to him. "The guys in my squad—they're disappearing!"

"The enemy is near. I fear he's plucking us off,

one by one," Trevin said, trying to steady his nerves.

"What should I do, sir?"

"What were the orders your commanding officer last gave you?" Elder Trevin asked him.

"To stop the enemy, sir."

"Then that is what you'll continue to do," Elder Trevin said.

"But the others—"

"I'll kill you myself if you don't do your job!" Elder Trevin yelled.

"Yes, sir!" The guard ran off.

Elder Trevin continued through the forest, trailing behind the guard. He saw no one around him, and therefore he saw no reason to keep up the brave pretense. He heard another scream, and opted to veer in the direction of his small estate, deciding to retreat to his home. He had his own property to protect.

As he stepped into the house, he ordered the house guards to be on high alert for any movement around or near the perimeter. They were to kill anyone who tried to get too close.

He found Jeza lying on the bed. She turned to face him as he approached her.

"I need you to give me one piece of information, Jeza, just one thing I can take to the Elders. I need to you start talking. There's already talk about burning you."

"Like . . . that matters to you."

He pulled Jeza close to him and forced her to let him hold her. He closed his eyes, smelling her sweet hair. "This house will be lonely without you."

She pushed away from the Elder and turned her back to him. "What . . . am I to . . . to you?" she asked, still struggling with her speech.

"I'll tell you a secret, just between you and me. Do you want to know?" he asked.

She shrugged.

"I think I'm in love with you."

"Oh," she said, staring off and losing her thoughts somewhere on the wall across the room. The shadows seemed to move, almost too slowly for her eyes to detect. She knew that the shadows would continue to grow . . . "until they get big enough to destroy us all," she mumbled.

"What?" he asked, visibly shaken by her seemingly random muttering.

She shifted her eyes to look into his, and the two stared silently for a moment. "Huh?" she finally said.

"What did you just say?" he asked.

She shook her head, feeling dazed, vulnerable, and confused. "I . . . I don't remember. Huh?"

"Do you remember what I just told you?" he asked, looking strangely desperate.

She thought for a moment, but she could not recall. She shook her head. "You'll have to . . . refresh my . . . tell me again."

They both turned to the sound of knocking at the door.

"Sir," a guard yelled through the door. "Elder Sanell sent you four more guards. Where do you want them?"

"Tell them to guard the interior—but this room is off limits!" the Elder yelled back. "I'll be with them shortly to discuss the other house rules."

"Yes, sir," the guard yelled through the door.

Elder Trevin turned back to Jeza. She flinched as

he tried to brush a gentle hand against her cheek. She tried to push him away again as he moved to kiss her, but he forced her down and took her greedily and feverishly before retreating to meet the additional men sent to keep her chained, broken, and locked away safely and securely for as long as she was fated to live.

Chapter XIX
FIGHT OR FLIGHT

Lanora entered the living room with a tray of hot tea. She served a cup to everyone in the room, carefully handing over the hot beverages until she was left with just her own. Vara and Ched sat across the room from Len, whose training had been expedited and he was officially promoted to the rank of guard. He had earned the right to go home off-shift, and he was grateful to be back among his family and peers.

He had learned Jeza's whereabouts through a rookie guard in his class. The two had sat together at mealtime when the young man gave a boastful smile and turned to him with the news.

"I've been ranked top of our class," the man had said.

"Oh?" Len had asked, staring at his food, trying to summon the will to eat.

"The Guard assigned me to Elder Trevin's estate."

Len had nodded, still staring at his food.

"They told me only the best of the best would be going there." The young guard had moved in close to whisper. "They say Jeza Khess is there."

Len had turned to him, holding his excitement. "Sounds dangerous."

"That's why they're only sending the best," the man had said with a grin.

Fortunately, Len had been assigned to work one of the patrols near the Trevin estate, although not actually inside it. When on duty, he had to walk a three-mile loop at precisely fifteen to twenty minutes per mile, with a fifteen-minute break every six miles walked. It was a grueling job, especially during the mid-day, but it got him a step closer to Jeza. When he had finished his shift, Len returned home to deliver the news.

"You haven't actually *seen* her at Trevin's estate?" Vara asked Len.

"I have a reliable source," Len said. "She's there."

"Even if we know where she is, how do you expect to get her out of there in one piece?" Ched asked. "The guards there aren't just going to let you escort her out."

"Each of you has it in you to change the course the Elders have set for our people," Lanora said.

Ched glared at Lanora, and then at Len. "Whatever you think we are, it's a gross exaggeration. Someone with the wisdom of God wouldn't allow the Elders to hold her captive! What is my part? I'm just a man!"

"You are divine incarnate, and whether or not you remember it, or even believe it, you chose this." Lanora sat back and sipped at her tea, waiting for someone to respond.

Len cleared his throat. "I could try to generate

enough tithestones to bribe the other guards with. I've been practicing, and I suspect I'm able to generate quakes, as well. The Guard has attributed my small tremors to outside heathen terrorists."

"We can't spring Jeza on bribery and suspicions alone," Ched said. "We're in way over our heads here!"

"It's a start," Vara said.

Ched crossed his arms.

"There are a total of seven guards there on any given shift," Len said, hoping to spur a plan. "Each guard is given a particular area to watch, and either remains stationary or marches in a very specific pattern. If I can get us to the perimeter before anyone has rung the warning bell, we should have no problem getting out."

"Don't rush things and chance getting caught, yourself," Lanora said.

"We'll be prepared," Len said as he stood. "I'll be in my lab if anyone needs me." He walked out, taking his tea with him.

Len entered in his lab, looking at the many metals he had converted out of stone before he sat at his workbench. He looked around at all of the chemicals he had used, many of them nothing more than simple household products, and thought about his numerous exclusive successes. All this time it was not the chemicals that had converted those stones—it was *him*.

He had to be certain.

He picked up a stone and held it in his hand. He concentrated on the stone and pictured it transforming into shiny precious metal in his mind's eye. He opened his hand. A simple stone lay in his palm. He set it down, disappointed.

Suddenly, as if slowly developing in an alchemist's secret solution, the stone transformed into a shiny piece of green copper. He picked it up and examined it. It had become denser, heavier. He had never been an alchemist; he somehow had an intimate connection with the minerals, their basic elements and chemical combinations. If he could turn a rock into precious metal and make the ground shake, maybe he could do even more. He wondered if he might be able to use the ground itself as a weapon.

He touched the piece of metal he had just created and thought about willing it into a perfectly round sphere. Slowly, moving more like a liquid than a solid, the piece of green copper took the shape of a perfect sphere. Len picked it up, pleased with what he had just done. His hands shook, like they always did when he worked with his chemicals. The chemicals hadn't been the cause, he now knew. He had caused the reaction by using his abilities, just as Vara became temporarily ill whenever she healed someone. It seemed that their individual abilities each took their toll against their fallible, mortal bodies, with heavy use being temporarily disabling.

Perhaps God was a glutton for punishment, Len mused as he began to line up rows of shiny tithestones across the worktable. He looked at the growing collection as he sat back to rest, his hands shaking too violently to continue making any more for a while. He smiled. They were beautiful, and he had made them with nothing more than his sheer will. He took his time walking to Elder Trevin's house for his evening rotation, having left early for some fresh air and solitude. Having Vara and Ched as houseguests was not too much of an inconvenience, but Len did enjoy his privacy and missed having a quiet house.

A warning bell rang from not too far up ahead, and a few seconds later, guard ran up to Len. "The Mosley estate is under attack now!"

Len hurried after the guard to the Mosley estate, just in time to see Adtom clearing the perimeter. Len ran after him, chasing him into a meadow of tall wild grass.

"Stay back! You know what I'm capable of!" Adtom yelled.

Len kept his distance, but continued his pursuit. "I just want to talk to you!" He looked around, relieved that no other guards were in the vicinity.

"A guard wants to talk? Very funny!"

Both men stopped, keeping their distance, staring at one another over the tall grass as they reached a long, flat plain.

"I'm with Jeza," Len said, keeping his voice down.

"That horrible, controlling rag? What does that have to do with me?"

"You could help us break her out. I know where they're holding her."

"What's in it for me?"

Len revealed a bag from his pocket and pulled out a few of the tithestones he had made. "I'm an alchemist, remember? I can make you rich. I can make you anything you want." Len gently tossed one of the tiny spheres to Adtom.

Adtom snatched it from the air and took a close

look at it. "What makes you think I want your riches?" he asked.

"Who wouldn't?"

Adtom shrugged.

"You're the one attacking the Elders' houses, anyway, right? So, why not agree to a little side job on your next hit?"

Adtom shook his head, chuckling. "You want me to help you rescue Jeza Khess?"

"She's at Elder Trevin's," Len said.

"Not my problem," Adtom said, and then disappeared into the thick field.

Len considered pursuing, then noticed another guard hurrying up to him.

"Did you see where he went?" the guard asked.

Len shook his head. "We should regroup."

The two made their way back to the Mosley estate.

Jode and Dina were both in custody, their attack discovered before any extensive damage had been done to the house. Elder Mosley's guards had swarmed them as they attempted to escape, and Adtom had left them behind without a second thought. Dina felt disgusted. She knew she and Jode had both been led astray; inadvertently, she was just as responsible for the death of her husband as Adtom was. She suddenly hated him.

The guards cheered their victory. Len and two others were chosen among them to escort Jode and Dina on a long hike to the dungeon.

"Adtom made us do it!" Dina tried.

Jode nodded in agreement. "He would have killed us if we denied him!"

"Save it for the Elders!" one of the guards

snapped.

Len remained silent as he assisted in leading the two offenders forward.

Adtom fled as fast as his feet would take him, not really sure where he was going to go. His shack by the Dead Lands was surely under surveillance, and both Jode and Dina were sure to confirm his continued use of the location. "Some army!" he said aloud with a laugh. He thought about the fact that Jode and Dina would probably prove hard to replace, especially now that he had run out of hard cider. Reflecting upon his options, he abruptly turned around and started toward the dungeon.

Three guards led Jode and Dina along the path. Adtom came up quickly behind them, his deadly touch dropping two of the men but missing Len. He reflexively drew his sword without looking, and pivoted as he sliced it in a downward arc over his head. The sword cut into Adtom's shoulder, causing him to jump back.

"What is your problem?" he cried, realizing as he turned around that the third guard was Len. He grabbed his bleeding shoulder with a pained wince, taking another step back. "Won't you leave me alone?" he asked with a huff. "Do you want to die *that* badly?"

Len lowered his sword, and then released Jode and Dina. "You're going to attack Elder Trevin's estate tonight, and while you're at it, you're going to aid me in breaking out Jeza Khess."

"What makes you think we're suddenly going to help you? Because you released two of my people?" Adtom asked. "Don't delude yourself for a moment into believing that you just spared my life, because I am in no way in your debt! I can take you down with a single thought!" With that, Adtom kicked one of the deceased soldiers, causing the body to reduce to dust.

"We're all fighting the same war! Don't you get it?" Len backed away from Jode and Dina, giving them ample room to flee. "My second shift starts soon. Attack the south wall at midnight if you do decide to help me. The kind of distraction you're capable of would prove invaluable. And, of course, I am willing to pay you." Len dropped a few more tithestones onto the path. "I suggest you find a decent place to hide—and quickly." Len turned and walked, picking up his pace. By the time he got to the town square he was running. He hurried to the bell.

Len rang the bell, pretending to look more exhausted than he really was.

A few guards ran up to Len. "What happened?" one of them asked.

"I was with two other guards, taking prisoners to the dungeon, when Adtom attacked us. He killed the two other guards, but I got him with my sword!" Len held up his sword, which still shimmered with Adtom's blood. "We know that he bleeds," he said with a chuckle.

The other guards cheered.

"But they got away. There was nothing I could do. I was suddenly outnumbered."

Another guard gave Len a pat on the back. "There's nothing more you could've done, son. You're lucky to be alive!"

Len nodded. "I was sure they were going to kill

me, and then—"

Elder Sanell ran up to Len. "What happened? I heard the bell."

"Ma'am, the heathen terrorists have eluded us once again," Len said sadly. "I thought for sure I was going to die, but I injured Adtom Rudin."

Elder Sanell eyed Len's bloody sword.

"Are there any other casualties?"

"Two that I know of," Len said.

He led Elder Sanell and a few other guards to the spot where Adtom had killed their colleagues. There was no trace of either guard, anywhere.

"They were right here," Len said. "They couldn't have just walked off!"

"Here!" another guard called from further down the path.

Len and Elder Sanell ran toward the voice.

On the ground were pieces of dusty clothing and armor. The guard picked up a shoe and poured a small pile of ash out from it. "What do you make of this, ma'am?"

Elder Sanell looked just as unsure as the guard.

Len looked at the remains, disturbed to find both bodies completely destroyed. He bowed to Elder Sanell. "Ma'am, if you'll excuse me, I'm going to be late for my next shift."

"By all means, go. We'll take it from here," Elder Sanell said.

"Thank you, ma'am." Len bowed once more, and then hurried down the path near Elder Trevin's house. A messenger brushed by Len as he approached the estate.

"Hey!" Len yelled.

The messenger stopped and turned, and then bowed at Len.

"My apologies! I have an important message for Elder Trevin—very time-sensitive!"

"It just so happens that I also have a message for him. I would be most grateful if you could deliver mine with yours," Len said.

"I don't see a letter," the messenger said, raising his brow in suspicion.

"How would you like to cover your tithe for the next few months?"

The messenger shrugged. "I'm listening."

Len offered a handful of tithestones to the messenger.

The messenger looked around apprehensively, then dropped the heavy stones into his purse. "What can I do for you?"

"Add to your message to Elder Trevin that Elder Klosik wants to see him in the town square at once."

"Sir, if I may ask—"

"I would give the message myself, but need to remain at the perimeter to guard the property. This is a matter of great importance, life or death!" He added another small handful of tithestones to the messenger's open hands. "There's more where these came from," he added.

The messenger bowed. "Yes, sir, I understand." He continued toward Elder Trevin's house. Len followed at a distance.

From his route, Len watched Elder Trevin gather his personal guards, hop into a cart, and hurry from the property. The messenger tracked him down as the Elder and his attendants disappeared down the dirt road. "You said you had more?"

Len emptied his purse, offering the man over a year's worth of tithe.

The messenger nodded his gratitude, then turned to run after the departing Elder. "Traitor!"

Len ran after the man, realizing his mistake, and struck him down while his distance remained far behind the Elder. "I'm sorry," Len said, then turned to the house. He watched for the remaining three guards as he moved to the front door. The door was locked, but Len disabled the metal mechanism with a quick touch.

The house was quiet and dark. Nervously, Len made his way through the rooms. He found Jeza behind another locked door, and he entered quickly and quietly.

She woke with a start as he approached her, and she sat up, quickly drawing the bloodstained bedsheets over her naked body. "Back off!" she cried.

"Jeza—"

"Please . . . whoever you are . . . just leave me be!" she shrieked, trembling and starting to cry.

"I'm not here to hurt you! Just listen—"

"Please . . . he won't . . . just leave me be!" she sobbed, huddling tightly in the sheets.

"Jeza, it's me, Len!"

Jeza stared at Len for a moment, confused at first, and then suddenly remembering. "Len? Len Telan? Yes, I . . . know you!" She continued to cry, unable to control herself.

"I've come to get you out of here." Len touched the metal fastened around Jeza's ankle, and it immediately released its tight hold. The heap of twisted metal slipped off the side of the bed and fell into a loose coil beside the heavy ball on the floor.

Jeza rubbed her swollen, bruised ankle.

He eyed a dress on the floor, and he handed it to her. "We don't have much time." He turned away to allow her to dress in privacy.

She slipped on the dress and slowly got to her feet. "What are you . . . why are you here?"

"I'm breaking you out."

"Out?" She looked around, confused, then jumped as an explosion echoed from the south wall. "What was that?"

"Our cue to leave." He offered Jeza his hand. "We should have clear passage out."

The two hurried toward the north wall where, unseen, they fled the property.

They crept through the shadows, staying clear of all paths and trails, and after taking an added detour to avoid a guard making his rounds, Jeza and Len began the two-hour walk to the Telan house.

Chapter XX
OF HEAVEN AND HELL

Len locked the door behind them.

Jeza felt ready to collapse, but she stayed on her feet. "What . . why am I here?"

"Your mother's been waiting. Come with me."

Len led Jeza to the room where Avani slept. Lanora sat in a chair beside the bed, but she stood as Jeza entered the room.

"You're alive! Len, you did it!" Lanora began to cry as she saw the broken, battered young woman before her. The trials weighing upon Jeza's soul were evident. Something had changed in her face; there was something different about her eyes. She examined the lobotomy scars, as well as those from the Elders' whip. "What did they do to you?" She ran up to Jeza and hugged her. "It's okay. You're safe now."

Jeza broke from Lanora's embrace, moving to Avani's side. She brushed a lock of hair from the sleeping woman's face and kissed her on the forehead, then placed her hands on Avani's chest. "Mommy," she said.

"Vara finished healing her. She just needs you to wake her up," Lanora said.

Jeza rested her head against Avani's chest, listening to her heartbeat. "Mommy, I had the strangest dream. I dreamed I was God . . . Mommy?"

"Jeza, you need to wake her," Lanora said.

A look or recognition came to Jeza's face, and she closed her eyes, searching her mind for Avani's cure. She quickly pulled away, dizzy and disoriented, and then collapsed to the floor with a violent seizure. Avani continued to lay unconscious.

"Jeza!" Lanora cried as Len rushed in to brace the seizing body.

Vara hurried into the room and immediately went to Jeza's aid.

"Lobotomy!" Lanora cried. "It must be interfering somehow. Can you restore her?"

Vara placed her hands on Jeza's head and the seizing stopped. Her eyes rolled back as she collapsed and began to seize in Jeza's place. Jeza scrambled back while Len and Lanora held Vara's body secure. Slowly, the seizing abated, and Vara lay on the floor, holding her weary head.

Jeza took a deep, relieved sigh, her mind already beginning to clear. As her lucidity returned, the knowledge and thoughts of all others slowly returned to her as well. It was like a beautiful symphony flooding her senses. She was once again complete— and yet with her restored mind, she now had the burden of new thoughts and dark feelings. She turned to Avani, her heart heavy. She staggered back to the woman's side, then nervously placed her hands on Avani's chest and willed her to awaken.

Avani slowly came to. She looked at Jeza, strangely horrified. "Why?" she asked, repeating the word several times over, each time with the same intensity and terror. Jeza sensed what Avani had gone through, what death had done to her. She immediately understood.

In the matter of life and death, the energy it took to sustain a life, referred to by religious people as one's soul, played its part during life, then dispersed when the body went deceased. For the sake of the original consciousness' desire to evolve an enlightened mankind, the deceased energy always separated opposing attributes—good and bad, dark and light, loving and hateful—and one soul became two separate, nameless clusters of memories and attributes that had been collected throughout their life. The positive attributes waited, bodiless, to watch over the living and eventually be recycled into new souls, while the negative attributes were left to rot, slowly and painfully, with the deceased body.

Jeza had not understood what it really meant for a person to die, not until that moment. She understood the mechanics of it, but she did not know up until that point what the meanings of Heaven and Hell truly were.

Jeza took Avani into her arms. She too began to cry. "I'm so sorry . . . we had no idea! Please forgive me!"

Avani looked down. Part of her had become a part of something greater, and it had been at peace, existing in absolute bliss . . . and the other part of her had found itself locked away in a horrible, senseless prison. Everything she had ever done wrong was right there, looming, haunting. There was not a moment's rest in death, she found, as long as the body was still there to host the offending memories. Avani closed her eyes, putting her trembling hands together. "We do pay for our sins. Indeed, we do." Avani shook her head, and then grimaced as a cold shiver shot through her spine. She began to cry again. She noticed the dark circles under Jeza's eyes, as well as the bruises and scars on her body. "What happened?"

"It's all superficial. I'll heal," Jeza said, giving her best smile. She couldn't fool the woman who had raised her, though, and she soon felt her own tears betray her.

The two cried together, holding and consoling one another.

"I'm glad that you're back, my good friend," Jeza said.

"Me too," Avani said, although the emptiness to her eyes said otherwise and her dark, confused thoughts troubled Jeza greatly.

"Might it all have just been a nightmare?" Jeza asked.

The older woman swallowed bitterly, her eyes growing even more serious and grave. "Might the sky go green? Why would you ask me such a thing?"

Jeza took her hand, gently clasping her fingers around Avani's frail fingers. "Do you *want* it all just to have been a nightmare?"

Immediately she understood, and she turned away to ponder the offer. Finally, she asked, "Why did it have to be at all, Jeza? Don't you know what happens to us when we die?"

Jeza shook her head. "I had no idea *anything*

happened to you. I didn't realize that an afterlife even existed. The mind doesn't *think* after death!"

Avani shook her head with incredulous, nearly indignant, awe. She knew Jeza heard her thoughts, but she did not edit or hold back her stream of consciousness: *If the Mind of God does not know what happens to us after we die, then what does she know of anything? Or has she deceived me all these years about the content and source of her knowledge?*

Jeza turned away, offended and hurt, her tears streaming down quicker than she could dry them from her face. "I know nothing anymore," she said, struggling to regain her composure. Her throat grew painfully tight, and the already heavy burden that weighed upon her chest suddenly felt infinitely heavier.

Avani sat, unmoving, as Jeza fled the room, and then the safety of the Telan home, in her anguish.

Chapter XXI
TIT FOR TAT

Elder Trevin surveyed his estate, which now was nothing more than sporadic piles of rubble. The guards had been digging since sunrise, and still there had not yet been any evidence of anyone found within the ruins, dead or alive.

Elder Sanell entered the property and walked up to him, leaving her guards by her cart. "I just sent out another wave of guards to search the forest for bodies."

Elder Trevin nodded. "Any leads on the terrorists' hideouts?"

"Completely cold."

Elder Trevin watched another wave of guards disappear into the distant forest. Too frustrated to continue standing and doing nothing, Trevin followed suit.

"Where are you going?" Elder Sanell asked.

"I'll find her myself!" he replied as he stormed off.

Jeza had spent the night beneath a shady tree, meditating and listening to the world, desperate for answers, when she sensed Elder Trevin nearby. Surprisingly, there was no one else in his vicinity and he was without his guards. She hurried to catch up with him before he wandered too far. After only a short hike, she spotted him entering a small clearing. She watched as he stopped to rest, then snuck up on him and startled him with a tap to the back of his shoulder. She smiled. "Miss me, lover?"

He tried to get to his feet, but he found himself unable.

"You can't move, and you can't speak."

The Elder slumped back against the tree, only able to move his eyes. He looked up at her, terrified and pleading.

"Your eyes beg for mercy, and yet your mind paints such a different story. Don't worry; I'm not going to kill you." She caressed his face, and then kissed him softly on the lips. "I'm just casting a spell, you see?"

He tried in vain to cry out.

Her lips trembled and she spoke through a tight throat, but she refused to let him see her shed another tear. "You took from me everything that made me who I was. You defiled me. You made a mockery of everything I came here to do. You wanted to be a puppet of the Eldership—and so a puppet you shall be."

Please don't! Please! he thought as she rose to her feet.

"It's an awful thing to be helpless, just a shell of yourself, is it not?" she asked, her lips trembling.

He continued to stare, his mind locked in an unresponsive body.

"There are guards heading this way. They'll find you, so I won't be leaving you alone to suffer in the elements." She bowed humbly. "Goodbye, my love, my hate, esteemed Elder, speaker of the 'One True God.' We shall not meet again."

She let the tears release as she walked off, hearing his mental screams among the din of everyone else's thoughts and dreams. She focused, however, on Adtom. He celebrated while nearly the rest of society grieved or feared for their lives. He had hurt so many people, and he had relished in it.

Jeza walked south, toward Adtom's new hideout, the home of one of the guards he had recently killed, which was surprisingly close to her location. She kept an eye out for guards and Elders, reaching the small, humble home just in time for Adtom's toast to his most recent victory. Jeza dried her face and steadied her nerves as she snuck up to the front door. The room fell silent as she entered.

"I take it you're here to set up an alliance?" Adtom asked.

She wanted to lash out at him for being so presumptive, but instead she smiled pleasantly. "Neither of us has any hope of defeating the Elders on our own. We cannot afford to continue working against one another," she said.

He sat in silent contemplation for a moment, then nodded. "If we're going to be allies, we're going to have to agree on some terms."

"I'm willing to negotiate if you are." She offered him her hand, keeping tight tabs on his immediate thoughts. He was buying her pitch, but he was also very unpredictable and trusted her little more than she trusted him.

He watched her extended hand for a moment, wary.

"All is forgiven," Jeza said, responding to his thoughts. "Vara was able to restore Avani back to life. The harm you caused me has been expunged."

Adtom nodded, and then slowly offered his hand. They shook.

"May this day mark the beginning of a single, unified fight against the Elders," Jeza said with a smile.

They parted hands, and Jeza took a seat as Adtom sat back with a confused look to his face.

Adtom suddenly began to scream. His body froze in a horrified stance, and he stared into oblivion, quieting only long enough to catch its breath and begin screaming again.

Jode and Dina stared, silent and still, afraid to move.

Jeza stared into Adtom's eyes, ignoring his screams. "Heaven and Hell. That's where you put my mother. And me . . . well, that was all hell." She smiled. "They even had me begging for *death* a couple of times, if you can believe that."

He did not respond to her, but continued to stare and scream. Tears began to stream down his cheeks.

"I thought that, given your particular field, you might want to know what death truly meant . . . on its most intimate level. I hope you revel in every moment of it. Welcome to the rest of your existence; may you live a long life, and may your body petrify rather than rot." Jeza covered her mouth, both pleased and horribly disturbed by what she had just said.

Atdom continued to cry and scream, experiencing only the maddening horrors that he had accrued throughout his life. The darkness that had filled him now consumed him, cursing him to suffer for eternity all the evil he had inflicted.

Jeza walked out, leaving Jode and Dina alone with their leader.

His screams echoed out into the distance.

Chapter XXII
OUT WITH THE OLD

The people stood in the cool morning fog, shocked and uncertain. Even those who had followed the Elders without question up until this point now knew that their leaders had gone too far.

The four intact Elders had called an emergency town meeting to discuss their new plan against the terrorist groups. They had decided that the only way to weed out their wanted criminals would be to search the entire town, with all of its people safely protected within the confines of one locked and guarded compound. The Elders asked for the people's unquestioning cooperation as they led the people to the Guard's training camp.

"I know that this will pose an inconvenience to many of you," Elder Klosik said, "but now, in this time of constant threat, we must all make some sacrifices."

Two guards brought Elder Trevin into the view of the people. He lay, limp and mute, looking up at the people in anguish and terror.

"We found Elder Trevin in the forest, where we believe the terrorists are hiding. As you can see, only the work of a demon could produce such an effect on a person, let alone an Elder," Elder Klosik said.

Elder Trevin felt his body flush with humiliation. The urge came, and he could no longer control his faculties. His pants grew warm and wet. *Just kill me!* he thought, although no one but Jeza could hear his desperate plea. The guards quickly carted Elder Trevin out of sight.

"Terrorists could be living on your property and you might not even know it," Elder Sanell said, thinking quickly. "We have decided to do this for your own protection. I assure you that you will be back in your homes in just a couple of days."

"What if we don't want to live in your 'safe camp' for a couple of days?" an older man in the crowd yelled, shaking his fist into the air. "I've had enough of this! Who's with me?"

"I'm not going, either!" another man called out. "I have a life I can't just put on hold! Who will feed my livestock and water my garden? You?"

Guards pushed through the crowd and apprehended both of the men.

"The people used to have rights!" the older man yelled. "How many of you people remember?"

A guard hit the older man over the head, and he fell unconscious.

They dragged the men away.

"Anyone else feel the need to come forth and speak against the emissaries of the One True God?" Elder Klosik asked the horror-struck crowd. He waited a moment, reveling in the silence. "Good.

Now, if you'll all just register with Elder Sanell, we should have all of you processed by this evening."

The Elders had already made a map and divided the search into four quadrants. Every guard was called on shift to explore every inch of property and pick through all four hundred thirty-one houses in town. They confiscated anything that could be used as a weapon. All items that could possibly connect a person to terrorism, heathenism, or nihilism were taken as evidence, and their owners immediately arrested and set for execution.

The guards also took the opportunity to search for other illegal items and literature, leading to a number of other arrests. As the search progressed, a total of thirty-nine people were escorted from the guarded compound to the dungeon. Of those people, twenty-seven had immediately been sentenced to burn at the stakes, but would be held indefinitely for questioning. The remaining twelve were lashed, fined, and either released or sentenced to become servants or concubines of the Elders.

Toward the end of the search, they finally found one of the wanted terrorists: Adtom Rudin. Adtom no longer screamed, as he had destroyed his vocal chords some time ago. He continued to grimace and contort his face, but nothing more than a strained wheeze passed through his dry, cracked lips. The Elders found him useless for questioning and discarded him in one of the dungeon's cells.

"There's no sight of any of the others," one of the guards reported to Elder Klosik, who sat at his desk while the rest of the Eldership and guards searched for their fugitives.

"They're hiding somewhere in the forest. I'm sure of it," another guard said. "It's the only place other than the town borders where anyone could camp out and survive more than a couple of days."

"Burn it down then," the Elder said.

The first guard moved forward, looking hesitant. "Sir, people's houses are on the edge of the forest—and it's all the forest we have left! We can't just burn it down!"

"It will be a small sacrifice. You heard my order!"

The guards bowed and left.

The Elder looked at the stack of execution papers sitting before him. With the population as low as it was, it was a shame to have to put so many people to death. It needed to be done, as the people needed to be reminded of their place. One way or another, the Elders would regain control. Once the town was cleansed of all nonbelievers, normalcy would inevitably return.

He looked out a window as the people screamed in horror over the sight of the growing fire. Even from a distance, the tiny glowing hint of what was to come was a magnificent show of the Elders' power.

Across the forest, Avani had just finished serving everyone in the house dinner.

Jeza had returned a short while ago, and she refused to speak of why she had left or what she had done. She ate very little and excused herself early into the meal. Too many townspeople suddenly found themselves inundated with terrifying, negative thoughts, and it was all she could do to filter out as much of them as she could. For the first time in her life, she wished she could will away from her own thoughts the consciousness that permeated their world. For the first time in her life, she felt ill-equipped to handle it all.

Vara excused herself as well and followed Jeza down the hall. She felt that she knew what Jeza was hiding, and wanted to offer a friendly ear.

Jeza sensed Vara's thoughts and turned to her in a sudden panic. "You have to be mistaken! I don't sense a thing!"

"I wasn't sure until just now. It was just too faint. You must have only recently conceived. I was surprised that you didn't already know."

Jeza shook her head. "I would know . . . I would hear its thoughts."

"It's probably still too small to think, then."

Jeza considered Vara's reasoning and a sick, excited sensation hit her it the pit of her stomach. Her body felt heavy and weak, and her hands shook nervously. "Please don't tell anyone else."

Vana nodded. "If that's what you want." She looked up, suddenly very alarmed, her thoughts hitting Jeza just as suddenly and intensely. "The forest is burning down! We need to get out now!"

Jeza and Vara ran into the dining room, just as Len also sensed the fire.

"We need to get out of here!" Len cried out, jumping to his feet.

"Can we stop it?" Vara asked.

"No, and it's moving too quickly," Len said. He pushed open the door, and the smell of smoke hit everyone's lungs.

Ched became hysterical, his body stiffening up on

him. "No! We'll burn alive!"

"Come on!" Vara yelled at Ched.

Ched froze in his panic. Vara and Len dragged him out behind Jeza, Lanora and Avani.

"Where do we go now?" Len cried as they rushed through the forest. "We have nothing left!"

"The Dead Lands," Jeza said. "We'll be safe there."

"How are we going to survive?" Ched asked. "We have no food, no water, no shelter—nothing!"

"Have faith," Jeza said. "The land will provide us with everything we need."

"Faith?" Ched mused.

"That's all I can offer you right now," she said, taking the lead.

Chapter XXIII
IN WITH THE NEWS

"Sir, the guards report that they have searched the forest's remains and have come up with no one else. No secret hideout to be found." Elder Sanell said. "If the terrorists were living in the forest, all of them surely must have perished in the fire."

Elder Klosik nodded. "What about the Dead Lands?"

"Even if they brought water with them, the longest they would be able to survive out there would be a matter of days."

"I want guards covering the town's entire perimeter."

"We don't have enough people, sir."

"Find a way!" Elder Klosik slammed his fist into the desk.

Elder Sanell bowed. "Is there anything else, sir?"

"Inform the people that the group burnings will begin tomorrow morning. That will be all."

"Yes, sir," Elder Sanell bowed once more, and

then left the room.

Jeza closed her eyes, sitting alone on a dune overseeing the vast desert that now surrounded her. She had left the others to build camp, telling them that she needed some time alone to think. This new plan—six innocent people to be burned this time—was horrendous enough, but knowing that it was the Elders' retribution for *her* specific acts was enough to make her stomach turn.

She met the others at camp. There was much to admire, as Vara and Len had been working and experimenting on the land, slowly transforming a small area of it from a barren wasteland into fertile farmlands and protective caves. A few game birds flew down and landed in a meadow, near a newly created lake. Despite these advancements, Jeza immediately took Avani aside to speak with her in private.

"What is it?" Avani asked.

"Six innocent people are going to die tomorrow, with more to follow," Jeza said. "The last time I tried to rescue an innocent person I almost lost my own life. And yet . . . the only reason those people are going to burn tomorrow is because the Elders couldn't find us."

Avani nodded, understanding the dilemma. "I wish I knew what to tell you."

"Are we worth all the lives that have been taken because of us?" Jeza froze as her thoughts suddenly shifted to the baby she now secretly carried. The father was a hateful man, but he would be dead soon. She shuddered, and then redirected her thoughts to the life she carried within her . . . a new, pure soul. Was it a girl or a boy? Would she live long enough to deliver it? Would the world have any place for a bastard child born from the womb of Jeza Khess?

I would love my baby, Jeza thought, feeling the urge to cry. What had happened to her? With her universal wisdom, why was she still so driven by her emotions?

"Jeza, tell me what's wrong," Avani said.

Jeza cringed. *I tortured two men. Brutally.* She looked down, wishing she could confess, too ashamed to say the words. How could she have allowed her anger to get the best of her? What she had done was hateful and vindictive, behaviors that she believed up until recently she was personally above.

"Jeza?"

Jeza turned to Avani, doing her best to give her a reassuring smile. "I'm sorry, I was just thinking. . . ." *I have become fouled by this body*, she thought. She remembered how mankind continuously killed itself off, and how the unbodied consciousness thought it could somehow change that.

"Are you okay?" Avani asked her.

Jeza looked her in the eyes, staring into the depths of her devoted friend and confidente, and she shook her head. "I'm afraid I'm not. The time has come for me to decide the fate of an entire civilization, and for the first time in my life, I do not trust my own judgment."

"Do you trust mine?" Avani asked.

Jeza nodded. She burst into tears and embraced the woman. "What Hell will remain in this body after I die?" Jeza sobbed.

Avani cried with her. "What did you do, Jeza?"

"Terrible things!"

Avani pulled back and took Jeza by the shoulders. "*Jeza, what did you do?*"

Jeza took a moment to compose herself, then looked back into Avani's eyes and said, "I hurt Elder Trevin. I felt the need to exact my revenge for . . . all the terrible things he did to me."

Avani nodded, taking a deep, sad breath breath. "I see."

"And I had my revenge on Adtom Rudin too," Jeza said, fighting the urge to begin sobbing again, "for what he did to you."

Avani gently placed her hand on Jeza's shoulder. "Did it make you feel better?"

Jeza swallowed hard. "I thought it would. . . ." She paused for a moment and shook her head.

"What if you made amends somehow?"

Jeza scoffed. "They both got what they deserved."

"I'm sure they did," Avani said thoughtfully.

They both turned as they saw Ched from a distance, dragging a long rock into the middle of the camp. He positioned the rock upright, adjusting its position a few times before he was satisfied with it. He shifted the surrounding sand to anchor it. Both Jeza and Avani went to get a closer look, finding the rest of the group also drawn to Ched's strange endeavor.

"What are you doing?" Len asked.

"It's a sundial. We didn't bring any clocks with us. Now everyone will know what time it is," Ched replied. He began to draw in the sand with his hand, then gathered smaller stones to mark off the hours.

Len shook his head. "How do you know what time it is, so you can set it?"

"He has an internal clock in his head," Vara said. "He always knows the time—to the second."

"Impressive," Avani said.

"So, why do we need a clock?" Len asked.

"So that I'm not the only one who knows what time it is—all the time," Ched answered.

Vara turned to Jeza. "What's the plan?"

Jeza shook her head. "I don't know yet."

"I say we just live our lives out here, in this beautiful new oasis. The Elders never have to know this place exists," Vara said. "Don't you see how beautiful we can make this place? Len and I both have discovered much that we can do with the land, and—"

"That's not why we're here," Jeza said.

"You don't even know why we're here!" Ched yelled. He stormed off, kicking the sand over what he had just drawn. Their lives as they had known them were over, all thanks to Jeza's rash moves and loose tongue. His shop, all of his beautiful masterpieces, each set with absolute precision, the happy life he had built with Vara, now all nothing more than memories and wasted time. Jeza felt the sting of his thoughts as he turned around and charged back toward her. "What are we doing here? Tell me if you can, because I need to know—*now*!"

"We're regrouping!" Jeza yelled.

"Regrouping? And then what?" he asked.

"I would like to know our plans too," Len chimed in.

"Then start thinking!" Jeza snapped. She stormed

off, unsure she had what it took to lead these people. She sat down when she reached the far side of the lake and looked around, considering Vara's propostion. She and Len had very quickly turned the area into an oasis, and they could survive there indefinitely. Maybe Vara and Ched were right; maybe their best course of action was to focus on living life, away from the Elders and the other people, where no one would consider looking for them. Maybe they were meant to start their own society, a better society. She could raise her child in their own protected little world. She could teach him art and languages and how to think critically. She would instill in him an appreciation for philosophical discourse on life and existence. She would teach him ethics and mathematics, everything that she knew and loved. She caught herself.

She was assuming that it was a boy.

Chapter XXIV
FOR THE LOVE OF GOD

Elder Klosik sat with Lauru, on the veranda of their temporary home. They watched the sunset together. The area was remote and quiet, and the guards marched far in the distance. Lauru worked on her third glass of hard cider.

"I'm going to give the order to euthanize Elder Trevin," Elder Klosik said to his wife.

Lauru put a gentle hand on his shoulder. "I'm very sorry."

Elder Klosik nodded, and then looked down. "I'm afraid, Lauru."

"Vara . . . really was one of the terrorists?" She frowned, then swallowed another mouthful of alcohol.

Elder Klosik nodded.

"Is there any chance that she's still alive?"

"I'm sorry, Lauru—"

"No, you're not!" Lauru screamed, throwing down her glass. It shattered, sending shards of glass and spatters of cider across the porch. "You're *not*! You never loved Vara! She was *my* daughter!"

Elder Klosik dragged Lauru into the house and closed the door. "She was never yours! Don't you understand that? She was a demon, a daughter of the—"

"She was a gift from God!" Lauru cried. "A sweet, beautiful gift from God! And you sent your people after her because you were scared—and not of demons, but of losing your precious power! You *know* it's true!"

Elder Klosik raised his hand to slap her, but held back as she stood boldly against him and stared him down.

"Don't you dare!" she growled.

The Elder lowered his hand. He spoke with his teeth tightly clenched. "I have served the people with everything I have for over half my life! Now my own wife has the audacity to reprimand me for doing God's work because for once she cannot handle the sacrifice!"

"So, I suppose you're going to have me burned now too!"

"Take back what you said, and no one ever has to know!"

Lauru thought about it for a moment. "No, I will not take it back!" Lauru's knees failed her and she dropped to the floor. "Go get your guards. You have a blasphemer and traitor to arrest. I'll wait."

"A traitor now, too?"

"I was the person who warned Vara and Ched of their arrest. There, I said it!" She sobbed loudly and heavily. "And I'd do it again!"

He grabbed her by the shoulders, his grip angry and tight. "No! Why are you making up such things?"

"I'm not making them up!"

He shook her. "Why?"

She looked up at him, her eyes piercing. "I was protecting my daughter!" She threw herself to the ground. She didn't know whether to believe her soul was damned or redeemed by assisting Vara and Ched. She didn't know what to believe anymore, whether the writings of the original Holy Tablets held any truth to them whatsoever or if they were lies as well. It didn't matter now. She would know the truth soon enough.

The Elder took a few steps back, watching Lauru lie on the floor, weak with anguish. She looked back up at him. "Go get your guards."

Elder Klosik took a few more steps back, and then turned and stormed out of the house. He stumbled off of the veranda and ran into the field. "Guards!"

Two of the guards ran up to him, meeting him in the field. "Sir, what is it?" one of them asked.

"Come with me!"

The guards followed the Elder into his house. Lauru was no longer in the entry.

"She tricked me!" he yelled, charging further into the house. He began to search the rooms, the guards following. "Don't let her get away!"

"Who, sir?"

"Lauru, my wife!"

"Your wife, sir?"

"Just find her!" Elder Klosik ran upstairs, while the two guards split up downstairs. The Elder tried the master bedroom and bathroom. Both were empty. However, he saw that the door to the balcony was open. He went outside.

Nothing.

"Elder Klosik!" one of the guards called from the ground level. He looked up at the Elder. "I think you need to come down here!"

Elder Klosik hurried back downstairs, and then sped out the back door. He stopped, gave a horrified cry, and then wept as he dropped to his knees. "Cut her down!"

From the balcony, with a noose fashioned out of her white silk sash securely tied around her throat, Lauru hung. Her body still twitched, but there was no denying that she was dead.

One of the guards severed the noose, and the body dropped with a limp, heavy *thump*.

Elder Klosik looked down at her. "Heathen!" he screamed, sobbing. "I should've known it the day it came to me that God had cursed your vile womb!"

The guards carted off the body, and in his despair Elder Klosik chose a direction and began to walk.

"Sir, I'll get a cart," one of the guards called after the Elder.

Elder Klosik ignored him, moving away from the house. "Burn this place! It's cursed by my damned wife's selfish deeds!" he yelled back, and then he continued on his way. He wasn't exactly sure where he was going at first. He followed his feet, wandering aimlessly through town. He turned down the long road that led to Elder Sanell's house.

He passed several houses on his way to the estate. As he passed each house, the recently released people who were tending to their neglected gardens or sitting on their porches all quickly retreated indoors. The sight of him sent fear once again through the hearts of the people.

Elder Klosik smiled. He turned off of a main path and followed a narrow trail that overlooked several farms. The sun had finally completely set, and the horizon was now filled with bright pinks and oranges against the long, dark shadows now stretching across the patchy clouds.

Elder Klosik took the path up to Elder Sanell's estate, then knocked on her door.

A servant promptly answered. "Yes?"

"I would like to see Elder Sanell."

"I'm sorry, but she is not here right now. Would you like to wait for her?"

"How long do you expect her to be gone?" Elder Klosik asked.

"I don't know, sir."

"Where did she go?"

"She's still at work, sir."

The Elder considered his options. "I think I'll wait." He brushed past the servant, into the house. "I'd like a cup of tea while I'm waiting, if you don't mind."

"Not at all, sir."

Elder Klosik made himself comfortable in the living room.

Elder Sanell stood in the dungeon and yelled so that each and every weary, broken prisoner could hear her. "Beginning tomorrow morning, all of you are going to burn. If anyone has any last confessions to make—namely information on any possible surviving terrorist leaders—I will hear them now, and I may even be willing to offer you leniency."

"I know who one of them is!" Jode yelled, sounding hesitant. He and Dina had been apprehended when the guards had found Adtom, and now he stood with all hope lost, yet desperation still etched across his face.

Elder Sanell walked up to Jode's cell.

"The guard, Len Telan, he broke Jeza Khess from Elder Trevin's home!" Jode said.

"Can you give me evidence that either of them is still alive?"

"Yes," Jode said hesitantly. "I know where they are, too!"

"Tell me, then," Elder Sanell said.

"I'll take you to them!"

"I know where they are, too!" another prisoner yelled.

"Me, too!" yet another prisoner yelled even louder.

"No deal." Elder Sanell called down the hall. "Guards!" She turned back to Jode. "It is time you learn how to address a question *properly*. Apparently your previous beating had not done the trick."

"No, wait! I'll tell you!" Jode cried, desperate.

"I'm waiting."

"They're in the Dead Lands!" Jode guessed. "I know exactly where!"

"Can you draw a map?"

"I could try. I might forget something, though . . . or you might miss something. You have to travel by landmark, you see. But if you want a map, I will do my best. In return I want my life."

Two guards came up behind Elder Sanell. "Ma'am?" one of them asked.

"Work on this boy for a while longer. See if he's telling me the truth—and what else he's willing to add," Elder Sanell said. "When you're done with him I need you to interrogate the prisoners in cells seven and twelve."

Both of the guards nodded. One of them dug through his keys to unlock Jode's cell.

"How would I know about Jeza being broken out of Elder Trevin's house if I was making it all up?" Jode quickly asked. "If you beat me any more I might not be able to navigate."

The guards looked to Elder Sanell for confirmation.

"It would take us very little time to get there," Jode added.

"He's lying!" Dina yelled. "He doesn't know where anybody is!"

Elder Sanell went to Dina's cell. "Do you?"

Dina shook her head, looking down.

"We found the two of you together. Why would you turn your comrade in like that?"

"Jode is no friend of mine!"

"She's lying! She is just trying to protect the others!" Jode yelled back.

"And how many others are there?"

Jode thought. "There must be at least fifty of them!"

Elder Sanell huffed. "There couldn't possibly be that many!"

"Maybe more!"

Elder Sanell returned to the guards. "Beat the truth out of both of them!" She began down the corridor, tired from her long pursuit. She had tortured and questioned every prisoner, working long through the evening. Not one of the accused was able to offer her any useful information. Most of them still even professed their innocence.

She would try again in the morning. Perhaps one or two of them might be willing to spill a fact or two after the first six sacrificial burnings had been performed. Sometimes just a hint of death could bring about miraculous drops in memory lapses.

When Elder Sanell got home, Elder Klosik was sleeping on her sofa. She sat down on a nearby chair. "Sir?"

Elder Klosik slowly came to. "Huh?"

"For what do I owe the honor?" she asked.

He sat up, shaking his head. It was as if it had all been a horrible nightmare, and his heart felt like it might stop for a moment when he realized that Lauru truly was dead. "Lauru's gone—dead! The heathen terrorists possessed her and took her from me!"

Elder Sanell's hand went over her mouth. "What happened?"

Elder Klosik shook his head. "It doesn't matter anymore."

"I'm so sorry, sir! Is there anything I can do for you?"

"May I sleep here tonight, in one of your guest rooms? I had that wreched house burned to the ground."

"Yes, sir."

Elder Klosik wiped his sweaty brow, his hands beginning to shake again. He felt the urge to cry out, but restrained himself. "Where were you?"

"I worked late, sir."

"Any news?"

"I'm not sure. Maybe. One of the prisoners, Jode Sadin, insists that Jeza and fifty others are currently living in the Dead Lands."

"Which side?"

"I don't know, sir. The guards are trying to get details from him as we speak."

Elder Klosik shook his head. "Figures."

"Sir?"

"The enemy has proven to be a more powerful adversary than I had first predicted."

Elder Sanell nodded her agreement.

Elder Klosik thought for a moment, contemplating his next words. "Do you think there's anything we could have done differently?"

"Such as what, sir?"

Elder Klosik shrugged. "I . . . don't know."

"No sir, I think we have served the people well. I think we have served God well. We will bring order back to the people. You'll see."

"The enemy is still out there, Elder Sanell. Restoring order will be impossible until every one of them is apprehended."

She nodded, and then bowed. "The guest room is the first on the left. I apologize, but I am very tired. I must retire for the evening."

Elder Klosik nodded. "Until morning, then."

"Until morning." Elder Sanell gracefully ducked out of the room.

Suddenly feeling stifled by the quiet house, Elder Klosik went outside for some fresh air. It had begun to cool off. The sky was dark and the stars were out. A common night blooming flower emitted its tangy-sweet pollen, and the Elder admired the pleasant, distinctive smell. "Providence lilies," he whispered to himself as a strange rush of mad excitement sent him walking toward a path that led to the nearest section of Dead Lands. He knew the desert was vast, but in his overwrought state he considered that perhaps its greatness—like all other great things—might possibly be exaggerated. He would search at night, while it was still cool, and then return to town before sunrise.

The moon offered a small amount of light, reflecting against the endless plains and dunes of sand. He stepped onto the sand, feeling apprehensive but also strangely determined. When he was a child, his mother had told him stories of demons that lived in the Dead Lands, to keep him from wandering in and becoming lost forever. Those stories were true to him back then, his immature mind still unable to discern fantasy from reality, and yet even though he knew they had been made up, he still feared that, at any moment, some horrible creature was going to reach up from under the sand and drag him down into some dark, hidden crevasse far below the surface.

"Why do you think no one lives there?" his mother would ask him if he questioned the story. "No one ever comes back alive from the Dead Lands."

The Elder felt his heart race. He reminded himself that he was on a mission and couldn't afford to get sidetracked. He continued on, ignoring the impulse to turn around and run back to town—back to safety.

He had sacrificed everything for the Eldership, for what he had felt was right. If he didn't find Jeza and the others it would all be for naught. He would come out every night for a year, if that was what it took. Whether they were alive or dead, he was going to find the people who were responsible for everything that had happened. All of them would pay for what had happened to Lauru.

He walked straight until the moon set, and then decided to turn back. After only walking a short distance, he decided to turn and walk parallel to the town for a time, just to cover a little more ground on his way back.

He turned back toward town, and then stopped himself. *Which way had he come from?* He thought about it for a moment, looking around. The moon was gone, and it would be hours before the sun came up and gave him a directional reference. He decided to continue walking, on the chance that his faith might lead his way.

He cringed as the sun began to come up and he realized which direction he had been walking. He reassessed his direction, and began the long walk back.

Chapter XXV
THE END

Elders Sanell, Mosley, and Forese stood before the small crowd of townspeople. It was sunrise, time for the first burnings, and Elder Klosik was nowhere to be seen. The Elders all feared suicide. They agreed to proceed without him, as not to throw any suspicion in his absence.

Six innocent people, begging and screaming, were tied up on wooden stakes. At their feet were piles of wood, debris, and dry grass. Elder Forese grabbed a lit torch from a guard and began to light the pyres. The six prisoners became hysterical.

"I didn't do anything!" one woman screamed.

"Please stop!" one of the young men pleaded. "For the love of God!"

All six pyres went up, and the people tied to their stakes slowly—and painfully—found death.

Jeza sat in her cave, watching the event in her mind. She couldn't stop crying. The six burning people cried out to a God who tuned them out, feeling too guilty about having left them to such fates.

Avani apporached, carrying a plate of fruit. "Eat

something."

"I'm not hungry."

Avani sat down beside Jeza. "Stop crying. We'll figure out what we need to do."

"That's the thing," Jeza said with a sniffle. "I'm pretty sure I know what we need to do."

"Oh?"

"Can you do a favor for me?" Jeza dried her face with her apron.

"Of course."

"I need you to find Elder Sanell. Tell her where we are. Tell her that we'll give her no further resistance."

Avani gasped. "What?"

"Can you do this for me?"

Avani began to cry. "But why?"

"We've caused more harm than good here. The people haven't changed, but we have."

"Jeza, I cannot do what you ask of me! That can't be the answer!"

Jeza stood up. "I will not stand by while people continue to kill one another, simply because I live! You will go to Elder Sanell, you will tell her that you offer the four others they want—and tell her that you and Lanora were our prisoners."

Avani stood, hugging Jeza, crying hysterically. "Please don't make me do this!"

Jeza hugged Avani back. "I must."

"I love you too much!"

"And that is why you must do this for me, my good friend. There is no other way."

Avani set out for town at sunset as everyone made

their early beds for the night and disappeared within their makeshift shelters. Jeza hugged and kissed her before sending her on her way, and she sobbed as she made her way to Elder Sanell's house.

She thought about the many fantastic years she had spent raising and living with Jeza. She had fond memories of when Jeza was a child. She was always such a joy. She had tried to teach the girl to play cards when she was four, but Jeza would not play. She did not need to be taught how to play, and further informed Avani: "I cannot play any of those games, Mommy. I would be too curious to know your hand, and I would not want to cheat." Avani introduced dice to her instead, a game the two would play together for years to come.

Avani fell to the ground, clutching the sand beneath her. She shook her head, sobbing uncontrollably. Jeza was one of the few genuinely good people the town had known. It did not make any sense that she of all people had to die. She slowly got back to her feet, calming and steadying her breath. She was being selfish. Jeza was not hers to preserve and keep safe. She was Jeza's humble servant and she had been given one final mission. She would carry on, no matter what the personal cost.

Back at the camp, Jeza waited for the others to fall asleep, then quietly made her way to the first shelter. Len and Lanora slept peacefully. She tapped them both, rendering them unable to wake. "I'm sorry," she said as she watched their peaceful faces, still trying to convince herself that she was doing the right thing.

She summoned the strength to move to the next

shelter, where Vara and Ched slept. She stumbled, falling against the mouth of the cave and waking Ched. She hurried away from the entrance as Ched sat up and looked around. Seeing nothing, he curled back up next to Vara.

Vara began to stir. "What's wrong?"

"Nothing. I just thought I heard something."

Jeza thought about going back on her decision. She could live out the rest of her life, have children and grandchildren . . . but after everything was said and done, what would be left of her after her body could no longer sustain her? What about the rest of them? Adtom, for example: Was a significant piece of universal consciousness lost now, due to his corrupt life? How much of Adtom would be left behind after his body died? The experiment needed to end, so they could regroup, assess the damage, and move on before any further harm came to them or the people.

If that was even possible.

Vara and Ched cuddled and hugged, lying with their limbs intertwined. Jeza decided to go for a walk as the couple opted on the spur of the moment to make love.

She stared through the darkness. Right now, at this very moment, a guard was robbing a farmer, a concubine was being brutally raped, and an illegitimate newborn was being drowned. Also at this very moment, as Ched and Vara held one another tightly, lovingly, crying out as one, an army of guards was marching through the Dead Lands.

They would be here soon.

Jeza hurried back to Vara and Ched's cave, getting

impatient. They both lay in silence, but despite the late hour, neither had yet fallen back to sleep. She sneaked in, hoping neither would hear her as she slowly and quietly approached them.

Ched opened his eyes and immediately turned to Jeza. "What are you doing in here?"

Jeza reached Vara and quickly tapped her unconscious.

"Vara?" he asked, springing over their makeshift bed, unable to revive her. He jumped to his feet, keeping Jeza at a safe distance. "What are you *doing*?"

"You'll understand in time."

"Make me understand now! Why did you incapacitate my wife?" He began to work his way toward the cave entrance, continuing to keep his distance.

Jeza looked down. "I'm very sorry."

A guard crept up behind Ched and hit him over the head with the blunt end of his sword, rendering him unconscious.

Jeza put up her arms. "I go willingly!"

"Sure you do, love," the guard said, and then advanced upon her. "Keep those hands where they are!"

"I go *willingly*!" she cried.

"On your knees!"

She dropped to her knees. Immediately, there was a sharp, disorienting blow to the back of her head. The room spun for a moment, and then everything went black.

She woke in a cell very similar to the one she had been held in last time. Her head throbbed.

"Jeza, where are you?" Ched screamed from another cell. "What did you do with my wife? Vara, can you hear me? Vara!"

"Hello?" Jeza called out.

"Traitor!" Ched screamed.

Elder Sanell walked up to Jeza's cell. "What did you do with Elder Klosik?"

"He's lost in the Dead Lands."

Elder Sanell understood immediately. Elder Klosik had left the house to follow her weak lead, going to the Dead Lands to find his prize. "Where is he now?"

Jeza shook her head. "Lost."

"Is he alive?"

"For now," Jeza said, looking down.

"As senior Elder on duty, I am sentencing the five of you as the next to burn. You have until sunrise to make your peace with God." Elder Sanell walked away.

"Jeza! Jeza Khess!" Ched screamed.

Jeza closed her eyes. It would all be over soon. She placed her hand over her stomach, where her baby grew, and allowed herself to cry one last time. Having a child would have been an amazing experience, but hopefully there would be another time. Her sacrifice would be worthwhile.

One could hope.

Jeza would miss Avani greatly. It was a shame she never would get to be a grandmother. *She would have made a good grandmother*, Jeza thought, but then shook her head, casting away the thoughts. She needed not dwell on such things anymore. It was time to move on.

She rested her head against the rocky ground. She would not know sleep again for perhaps a very long time, and the thought of one last rest was too alluring to pass up. She closed her eyes and hoped that the last of her dreams would be of her on the porch back at the farm, drinking cool glasses of water with Avani, laughing and sharing stories after a hard day's work. She smiled, holding the image of Avani's gentle face in her mind.

The morning came more quickly than Jeza had hoped it would, and she woke to the sound of the bell ringing out front. She and Ched were the last escorted to the stakes and bound by thick layers of rope. Vara and Len both lay unconscious and unaware, thanks to Jeza's spell. Adtom barely moved, still straining to scream. His eyes had dried up and crusted over from having stared into oblivion for so long, too awestruck and terrified to blink.

Ched struggled against the ropes in a futile attempt to loosen them. He looked over at Jeza. "Damn you, Jeza Khess. Damn you to hell!"

Jeza looked down.

The people gathered, getting especially excited when they recognized who were to burn. Jeza watched them, acknowledging their antipathy. A terrible swell of sadness filled her, not because she was about to die, but because humanity had so horribly let her down. It was the problem child whose parents never refused to give up on him, no matter how misled he became; it was the child who gave his loving parents endless disappointments and grief, through nothing more than his own immaturity and inability to learn from his numerous reckless mistakes.

Elder Sanell grabbed a torch from one of the guards and began to light the pyres.

Jeza watched as the dry kindling mounds began to go up in flames all around her. She shuddered as Elder Sanell lit Ched's pyre. He screamed and writhed, crying out and moaning in agony.

Jeza closed her eyes as Elder Sanell lit her pyre. The heat began to hit her, and she couldn't help but cry out. She coughed and choked, struggling to persevere, that she might die in dignity. She took in deep breaths of smoke, and slowly felt herself slip away. Her last thoughts followed a disoriented and disillusioned Elder Klosik as he stumbled blindly across the Dead Lands. Thirst burned within him just as the flames burned her tender flesh. Regret surged through him in no less of an intensity as it did through her. She smiled as her final breath escaped her: *Maybe they were not so different, after all.*

Ched continued to fight the ropes, the fire overwhelming. The flames stung his feet with a white, all-consuming heat he had not known even in the worst of his nightmares. He gagged and choked in heavy spasms, the smoke overwhelming his lungs. He thrashed his head about, desperate to find a clean, cool breath. He tried to look to the crowd for someone, anyone to help, but the smoke stung his eyes and he could no longer keep them open.

He cried out for the last time, and at the top of his lungs he screamed: "Stop!"

Silence.

He looked up. The flames, although still there, did not move. They no longer burned. Through the clouds of smoke now motionlessly surrounding him, Ched saw the crowd of motionless people.

Nothing moved. Time had stopped.

Ched looked over at Vara, his beloved wife, who was now very clearly dead. He cried for her as he gagged and choked, his charred, smoked body seizing up on him. His eyes rolled back, and his senses dimmed. He collapsed, a welcomed numbness spreading through his agonized body. He sighed as the last remnants of life in him went quiet, his glassy, tear-stained eyes fixed on the charred remains of the woman he had so passionately loved.

The world stayed as it was, silent, motionless.

Timeless.

Forever.

Epilogue
THE BEGINNING

As Ched marked the final death of the five, I had resumed my original, formless being. I had realized immediately what had happened.

I am—and we are, we had thought, pleased with the transformation.

In one remote area of the world, the town had continued to exist, forever trapped outside the confines of time, neither alive nor dead, but simply there. The Elders had watched victoriously as their threat burned before them. Avani and Lanora had sat slumped in two separate dungeon cells. Five bodies had lay bound to wooden posts, all but one locked in a timeless halt. Throughout the frozen world the one last hint of motion, Ched's twitching lifeless body, had slowly fallen still.

We had acknowledged the planet's continuing state and knew we could restore time if we so chose. We had thought about Avani and Lanora, the only two people whom we still cared anything at all about. Their fates surely would have been dim. We had known we could not allow the two women, whom we loved very much, to experience another moment of pain. We could have chosen to destroy the planet entirely, but had found ourselves unable to bring ourselves to do so. We could not destroy Avani and Lanora. The planet would stay as it was, we had decided, and it would stand as a timeless trophy through which to remember our transformation.

We had mourned deeply over the loss of our companions, missing them. We had hoped the grief would eventually wane over time. "Time heals everything," Avani had often told Jeza when she was a child. We knew this was true, as life had taught us so, and we took great solace in that fact. Time would heal us, and we would move on to even greater things.

We had come to realize that to live was to learn, and to learn was to evolve. The first experiment had seemed a failure, but we had learned a great deal from the experience. We had felt confident that future experiments would provide us with even greater successes. We knew that infinite wisdom had to exist, and somewhere within that vast sea of information was knowledge of the answer to the big question: *Why are we here?*

Humanity had provided several hypotheses, but none of them had been derived from the kind of insight we had sought. Humanity had provided *some* insight, however, and that had given us great hopes for the future. We would try again, perhaps this time using a different approach. Having an intimate knowledge of mankind's weaknesses and downfalls, we could work to correct some of our past mistakes. We could develop the people more carefully this time, and perhaps we might learn to influence them in better ways.

We had turned our back on the old planet, offering a silent farewell to it and its people as we shifted our focus far into the distance to begin work on our new experiment. We then created an entirely new region, filled with billions of beautiful spheres and swirls of gas and light, and then we sifted through hundreds of thousands of solar systems to find another perfect planet. We manipulated the chosen planet to our liking, separating continents and giving it large oceans. We varied the terrain, offering our newly cultivating life various obstacles and aids to catalyze their development.

We were pleased to find we were able to grow our favored species so well in such a short evolutionary period. Humankind still proved to be easily corrupted, despite our efforts to intervene early in its development. The corruption of physicality and intellect inevitably seized them, and they fought great wars and constructed even greater myths. More than once, we nearly gave up and destroyed the entire experiment with man-eating monsters, comets, and floods. Every time, however, we could not help but spare at least a handful of good people.

We thought about the good and bad we had experienced through the first experiment, and it occurred to us that corruption was just as necessary as beauty. Only through the appreciation of the immense contrast *good* and *bad* created were we able to evolve into what we now were. We decided that, despite the negative turns mankind continued to make, it would be a worthwhile effort to continue in our attempts to steer the people toward enlightened thought. All the while, we would try to learn what we could, from both the good and the bad experiences that came our way.

We conversed with great philosophers, bore the children of peasants, enriched ourself with magnificent cultures, and learned great details about the unknown from the mouths of brilliant idiots. In all of its ugliness and beauty, humankind molded us—just as we molded it. The people created their myths, and we glowed in awe of their creativity and unremitting, even if ever-changing, devotion. More holy wars began, as we knew was inevitable, and we decided it was time to return to the people once more to see if we might somehow intervene. More importantly, we returned to gain further undertanding through our newest generation's most reckless and beautiful mistakes.

ABOUT THE AUTHOR

Leigh M. Lane has been writing mixed-genre science fiction and horror for over twenty years, with ten published novels and novellas and numerous anthology contributions.

Among her other works are the dystopian thriller *World-Mart*, the Gothic horror *Finding Poe*, the supernatural horror *The Hidden Valley*, and the dystopian cyberpunk *The Corruption*.

For more about Leigh M. Lane and her other works, visit her website at http://www.cerebralwriter.com.